WITHDRAWN

A Garland Series

Foundations of the Novel

Representative Early

Eighteenth-Century Fiction

A collection of 100 rare titles
reprinted in photo-facsimile in 71 volumes

Foundations of the Novel

compiled and edited by

Michael F. Shugrue

Secretary for English for the M.L.A.

with New Introductions for each volume by

Michael Shugrue, *City College of C.U.N Y.*

Malcolm J. Bosse, *City College of C.U.N.Y.*

William Graves, *N.Y. Institute of Technology*

The Impartial Secret History of Arlus, Fortunatus, and Odolphus

Anonymous

The History of the Proceedings of the Mandarins and Proatins of the Britomartian Empire

Anonymous

The Adventures of Five Englishmen from Pulo Condoro

by
Walter Vaughan

with a new introduction
for the Garland Edition by
William Graves

Garland Publishing, Inc., New York & London

1972

The new introduction for the

Garland *Foundations of the Novel* Edition

is Copyright © 1972, by

Garland Publishing, Inc., New York & London

All Rights Reserved

Library of Congress Cataloging in Publication Data
Main entry under title:

The Impartial secret history of Arlus.

(Foundations of the novel)
The Impartial secret history ... is a reprint of the
4th 1710 ed.; the 3 previous editions, also of 1710,
were published under title: The Secret history of Arlus
and Odolphus, and have been variously ascribed to the
1st Earl of Oxford and to D. Defoe. The History of the
proceedings ... is a reprint of the 1712 ed. The
adventures of five Englishmen ... is a reprint of the
1714 ed.
   1. English fiction--18th century. I. The History
of the proceedings of the Mandarins and Proatins of the
Britomartian Empire. 1972. II. Vaughan, Walter.
The adventures of five Englishmen from Pulo Condoro.
1972. III. Oxford, Robert Harley, 1st Earl of, 1661-
1724. IV. Defoe, Daniel, 1661?-1731. V. Series.
PZ1.I46 1972 [PR1297]   823'.5'08   75-170521
ISBN 0-8240-0528-7

Introduction

The Impartial Secret History of Arlus, Fortunatus, and Odolphus *(1710) and* The History of the Proceedings of the Mandarins and Proatins of the Britomartian Empire *(1712) are representative of the allegorical satires which anonymous early eighteenth-century Whig propagandists directed against the Tories. Political allegories were extremely popular at this point in English history, but without assistance the modern reader is apt to miss both the pleasure and instruction these works once offered because of his unfamiliarity with the historical details that the books encompass. The following synopses of the books, with keys to the more obscure names, will help the reader view the works with the perspective of his eighteenth-century counterpart.*

The History of the Proceedings of the Mandarins and Proatins of the Britomartian Empire, *the more difficult of the books, tells of the havoc brought to Britomartia (Great Britain) by such men as Don Wilhelmino (William Bromley), Novicius (Robert Harley, Earl of Oxford), and Henrico (Henry St. John, Viscount of Bolingbroke), all supporters of the Montalti party (Tory High Church). Through trickery and outright fraud, these men gain the favor of the Empress Palatina (Queen Anne), who replaces her previously trusted ministers, men of*

5

INTRODUCTION

principle she has inherited from her predecessor the Emperor Aurantia (King William III).

Having gained control of the Proatins (House of Commons) in the 1710 elections and the Mandarins (House of Lords) through Palatina's "packing" of the chamber, these enemies of the state swiftly proceed against the true lovers of Britomartia. Prince Mirabel (the Duke of Marlborough), for example, is shorn of his military powers. Policy changes are effected as well. The proud tradition of sanctuary to foreign co-religionists is threatened; simultaneously, new churches are built for the Montalti; finally, and most seriously, secret negotiations are held with Lilliania (France), with whom the Britomartians are at war, in violation of Britomartia's treaties with her allies. Some of the other characters in the story are Mordamanno (Lord Peterborough), Galvacio (Earl of Galway) Luteolo (probably the Earl of Nottingham), and Achon (Prince Eugene).

The Impartial Secret History of Arlus, Fortunatus, and Odolphus *covers a larger span of history than the other work.* The Impartial Secret History *begins with the ascendancy of Jago Vulpecius (King James I) to the throne of Grand-Insula (Great Britain) in 1603. The author attacks Jago Vulpecius as a bungling would-be tyrant anxious to impose on his subjects the religion (Roman Catholicism) of Ausonia (Rome), Boetica (Spain), and Ludovisia (France). His son, Obstinato Bigottus (King Charles I), failing in his attempt to impose despotism on Thistellania (Scotland) and*

6

INTRODUCTION

Rosacia (England), loses his head at the hands of the Gerontes (Parliamentarians). Don Carlo Physcon (King Charles II), the third of this line of troublesome and incompetent rulers, trusts too much his treacherous brother Don Diego Idololatro (King James II), who, to please his foreign supporters, conspires to murder the king. Don Diego Idololatro's short reign is ended by the Gerontes who bring Auromalia (King William III) and Maria (Queen Mary II) to the throne.

The tranquility of Auromalia's reign is threatened by the Rapparies (predecessors of the Tories), who, at heart, are friends and agents of the fallen Don Diego Idololatro. Unfortunately, the king's death prevents him from replacing the Rapparies in the government with Philopatrians (Whigs). The remainder of the book is a plea for the present ruler Heroina (Queen Anne) to oust the Rapparies from her ministry. The author charges that the Rapparies have tried to prevent her rise to power, have maligned her friends, have engaged in internal political maneuvers to prepare the way for the Pretender, and have conspired with the Emperor of Ludovisia. Other names mentioned in the book include Strategomacarius (the Duke of Marlborough), Gazophilacius (Sidney Godolphin), Astutus (Robert Harley), Alectia (Abigail Masham), and Mitrato Exoniaco (Dr. Henry Sacheverell).

Works such as The History of the Proceedings of the Mandarins and Proatins of the Britomartian Empire *and* The Impartial Secret History of Arlus, Fortunatus, and Odolphus, *while lacking in full character and plot*

7

INTRODUCTION

development, were important in the development of the novel. *Forced by threats of present and future prosecution and encouraged by tradition to use the allegorical form, political propagandists in the early eighteenth century created relatively structured and realistic fiction that afforded their readers entertainment as well as instruction.*

Published in 1714, with Walter Vaughan, probably a pseudonym, named as author, the third work in this volume, The Adventures of Five Englishmen, *reflects the eighteenth-century English interest in exotic travel and adventure. From the time of the great Elizabethan explorations, English readers had numerous accounts purporting to describe the characteristics of people outside Western Europe:* Mahomet and Irene *and* Sultan Solyman *in William Painter's two volume collection* The Palace of Pleasure *(1566-7); Giovanni Paolo Marana's famous* Letters Writ by a Turkish Spy *(1687);* A Voyage to the New Island Fonseca, near Barbadoes *(1708); and Francois Maximilien Misson's* A New Voyage to the East-Indies by Francis Leguat and his Companions *(1708).*

The Adventures of Five Englishmen *follows one typical format of the genre. The reader learns first of a shipwreck, the ensuing confusion and suffering, then of the sighting of natives, the good and bad qualities of these people from the English vantage point, and finally the delivery of the sufferers that renders feasible the publication of the tale. This pattern enables the author to supply his reader with adventure and suspense as well*

8

INTRODUCTION

as philosophical and practical considerations on comparative national customs.

After the initial mishaps connected to their shipwreck, the sailors, for the remainder of the book, are concerned with the decidedly un-English qualities of the natives and with ultimately gaining passage to England. Characteristic of the people of Jehore, a portion of Indo-China where the sailors eventually arrive, is an occasional casual cruelty, an inclination to accept despotic rulers, relative ignorance, and the blind acceptance of Mohammedanism. The rulers of Jehore insist that their English captives convert, endure circumcision, and avail themselves of the benefits allowed to male Mohammedans. All but Vaughan waver in their English Christian faith, but through a variety of helpful circumstances, the sailors escape unscathed.

The Adventures of Five Englishmen, *representative of a wave of early eighteenth-century travel fiction which culminated in Daniel Defoe's* Robinson Crusoe *(1719), helped condition readers to the possibilities of a truly imaginative fiction.*

William Graves

The Impartial
Secret History of
Arlus, Fortunatus, and Odolphus

Anonymous

Bibliographical note:

*This facsimile has been made from a copy in the
Beinecke Library of Yale University
(College Pamphlets 355)*

The IMPARTIAL

SECRET HISTORY

O F

Arlus, Fortunatus, and *Odolphus,*

Miniſters of STATE, *&c.*

A

The Impartial
SECRET HISTORY
OF
Arlus, Fortunatus, and *Odolphus,*
MINISTERS of STATE
TO THE
Emprefs of *GRAND-INSULA.*

In which are Difcover'd,

The true and Juft CAUSES of the Removal of ARLUS, who by his T————s Ad-
————n, rather Deferv'd *H——n's* Pun————t,
than *Mordecai's* Preferment; And Juftice is done
to the Charafter of FORTUNATUS and
ODOLPHUS, and they prov'd to have dif-
charg'd Their Trufts with Equal Honour, Honefty,
and Succefs.

Humbly offer'd to thofe Good People of *Grand-Infula* who
love their Country, are not bigoted to a Party, and
blinded by the Fulfom Flatteries beftow'd on *Arlus* by a
Gang of Mercenaries.

---

*Qui Romæ faciam? Mentiri nefcio, Librum
Si malus eft, nequeo Laudare* ————

Printed in the Year, 1710.
(Price 6 *d.*)

The Impartial

SECRET HISTORY

OF

Arlus, Fortunatus, and Odolphus.

TIS now about 108 Years fince *Jago Vulpecius* King of *Thiftellania* fucceeded to the whole Empire of *Grand-Infula* ; He had a great deal more of the Fox than the Lion, tho' he carried the latter for his Enfign ; but he cover'd his natural Want of Courage under a ftudied Affectation of Peace, and made up by *Aufonian* Politics what he wanted of *Albanian* Prowefs. Having been interrupted in his Defign of fetting up a defpotical Sway over the rugged Boars of the *North*, he fancied he fhould more eafily accomplifh his End over the pamper'd Leopards of the *South*. He had a mighty Itch to be mending the Law and Gofpel, and to have both of 'em modell'd to his own Pallat. He knew the readieft way to effect this was to get all the Governors of *Eglifia* and *Leguleia* at his Beck, in which he made a great Progrefs, but now and then met with fome Rubbs in his Way by the ftubborn *Gerontes* of *Legiflatia*. To furmount this Obftacle, he kept a fecret Correfpondence with the Grand *Mufti* of *Aufonia*, and by his means hop'd to effect a Match

B   betwixt

betwixt his Son the Prince of *Grand-Insula,* and the Daughter of the Emperor of *Boetica.* To accomplish this, he made great Advances to reconcile his Subjects of *Eglisia* with those of the *Mufti* of *Ausonia,* but the Match with *Boetica* having miscarried; he obtain'd the Promise of another with *Ludovisia,* much on the same Terms. His Design in all this was to procure a powerful Alliance with some of the greatest Despots of *Continentia,* that he might by their Assistance overcome the *Gerontes* of *Legislatia,* and obtain an absolute Empire over *Grand-Insula*; but just as he was upon the Brink of Enjoyment, his unlucky Stars sent him out of the World by the Application of a certain Cataplasm that seldom fails in its Operation. 'Twas mightily suspected that some who got most by his Death, were not very careful to preserve his Life, and thus he made his Exit.

His Son *Obstinato Bigottus,* who had no less Inclination to the Constitution of *Turcomania* than himself, pursued the Plan, expres'd an open Contempt of the *Gerontes* of *Legislatia,* and being sure of the Governors of *Eglisia,* who were then in Confederacy with the Inhabitants of *Ausonia,* he made no doubt of establishing an absolute Dominion in *Grand-Insula.* The greatest Stop in his way was the Stubborness of the *Gerontes,* who being time out of mind possess'd of a Share in the Government of the Country, and absolute Masters of the Purse, would contribute nothing towards his Enterprize, being irreconcileable Enemies to a despotical Power and the Religion of *Ausonia,* which *Obstinato Bigottus* was oblig'd to favour, by the Engagement he was under to the
Mufti,

Mufti, and his Marriage Contract with the Princess of *Ludovisia*.

The Emperor of *Grand-Infula* being thus contradicted by the *Gerontes* of *Legiflatia*, invaded their Province, rais'd Money without their Consent, and being likewise affifted by the Purfe of *Eglifia*, refolv'd firft to eftablifh his fovereign and abfolute Empire over *Thiftellania*, but the ftiff-necked Inhabitants of that Country took Arms, ftood on their Defence, and brought *Bigottus* to Reafon. This animated the People of *Rofacia* the Southern, and by far the moft valuable Part of *Grand.Infula*, to infift likewife upon a Redrefs of their Grievances, which being obftinately refus'd by means of the Leaders of *Eglifia* and their Friends of *Aufonia*, fupported by the Authority and Intrigues of the Emprefs, a Daughter of *Ludovifia*, a Rupture enfued betwixt the Emperor of *Grand-Infula*, and his *Gerontes* of *Legiflatia*, who, tho' worfted by him at firft, did, by the Affiftance of the *Albanians*, prove too hard for him at laft ; of which, a prevailing Party in the Army, rais'd by the *Gerontes*, taking the Advantage, they invaded both him and their Patrons, and having diffolv'd the latter, cut off *Bigottus's* Head.

After a Government by the Sword, under the Conduct of an Ufurper for 10 Years, and about two more of Anarchy, *Don Carlo Phyfcon*, eldeft Son to *Bigottus*, fucceeded, with almoft the univerfal Confent of the People of *Grand-Infula*, who had great Expectations from him, in which they were unhappily difappointed ; for he brought home with him, tho' he diffembled it, the Religion of *Aufonia*, and the Politicks of *Ludovifia*, but being too cunning, or wanting Courage, to practife

them

them himfelf, he left that to the Management of his Brother *Don Diego Idololatro*, with the Affiftance and Advice of the High-flying Priefts of *Aufonia* and *Eglifia*. In the mean Time the Emperor *Don Carlo* fanter'd away his Time betwixt his Miffes and his Cups, while *Don Diego* mounted the Back of *Eglifia*, and rode full fpeed towards *Aufonia*.

The two Royal Brothers being warn'd by their Father's deplorable Fate not to come to a Rupture with the *Gerontes*, till they were in a Condition to act without them, they took the fafer way of buying them off with Bribes, by which they had well nigh eftablifh'd a defpotical Government over *Grand-Infula*: But their Cafh running low, and not being able to fatisfy all the craving Appetites, which haunted them every Day, they refolv'd on a new Way of Management, which was to make Application to the Emperor of *Ludovifia*, and the *Mufti* of *Aufonia*, to fupply them with Money, in Order to introduce the Politics of the one, and the Religion of the other. *Don Diego* being of a warmer Complexion, and more zealous than his Brother, the *Aufonians* grew impatient to have him on the Throne, and for that End confpir'd with him to cut off the Emperor, who in truth lov'd his Pleafures more than any Religion whatever; and an eafy Life rather than he wou'd venture to be forc'd to travel a fecond time, as his Brother brought himfelf afterwards to do by his precipitant Conduct. This Plot being difcover'd, the Inhabitants of *Grand-Infula* took the Alarm, and the Emperor, tho' acquainted with every Part of the Plot, but that againft his own Life, feem'd to be rous'd fo as to recover his Senfes, and to leave
the

the Enquiry into the Plot, to the Care of the *Gerontes.*

This put *Don Diego* with his *Aufonian* and *Eglifian* Friends into a terrible Fright; fo that for fome time he was fent out of *Grand-Infula*,more to fave him from Danger than to do the Nation Ju-ftice. The *Gerontes* in the mean time knowing him to 'be irreconcilable to their Religion and Liberties, endeavoured to exclude him from the Succeffion, but in vain; for the Emperor wou'd not hear of it, and the Leaders of *Eglifia* alledging it to be inconfiftent with their Princi-ples, influenc'd their blind Followers fo far as to baffle that Defign.

Don Diego and his Friends having efcap'd this Danger, he found means by affiftance of the Fu-riofos of *Elglifia* to turn the Plot upon the *Phi-lopatrians*, to whom they gave the reproachful Name of *Levellers*, and falfly appropriated that of *Loyalifts* to themfelves.

Matters being thus prepar'd, the Emperor was laid afleep by an *Aufonian* Potion, and *Don Diego Idololatro* mounted the Throne; he mightily ca-refs'd his Friends of *Eglifia*, who were weak enough to belive him, and to concur with him in all his Meafures while he perfecuted their Bre-thren of *Geneviaca*, and nothing was heard of be-twixt them but the greateft Endearments. Thus Things continu'd a while, but the Emperor's *Aufonian* Friends growing impatient for a Share of the rich Poffeffions of *Eglifia*, and thinking them-felves intitled to all the principal Pofts of *Grand-Infula*, they put him upon fuch Meafures as dif-oblig'd thofe of *Eglifia*, upon which their Leaders forgetting their former Doctrine, of Non-refift-ance

ance and Paffive-Obedience, they oppos'd the Emperor to his Face.

In Order to ftrengthen himfelf againft them, he deliver'd their Brethren of *Geneviaca* from their Perfecution, but with a Defign publickly to introduce the Worfhip of *Aufonia*, which was againft Law, on Pretence of fetting all his Subjects on an equal footing as to Liberty of Religion. The better to effect this, he erected a High Commiffion compos'd chiefly of the Furiofos of *Eglifia*, in order to turn out, and punifh fuch as wou'd not comply with his Meafures.

And that all he was doing might have a Shadow of Law, he refolved to have the *Gerontes* wholly compos'd of his own Creatures: To this End he compleated the Overthrow of the Conftitution which his Brother had begun, diffranchis'd all the *Ciudadas* of *Grand-Infula*, and reduc'd their Metropolis to a Village, that he might have the returning Officers all in his own Power; and to perpetuate the *Aufonian* Religion, and *Ludovifian* Politics, his Emprefs an *Aufonian* by Birth and Religion, trump'd up a counterfeit Male Heir, on purpofe to difinherit the Emperor's two Daughters, and their Pofterity, becaufe they were zealous for the true Religion of *Eglifia*, and had a perfect Abhorrence for that of *Aufonia*.

Matters being brought to this Extremity, and the Bigots of *Eglifia* finding that their elder Brethren of *Aufonia*, had by far the greateft Share of the Emperor's Favour, they cut the Throat of *Nulla Refiftentia*, alledged fhe was a fpurious Baftard, and not the true Offspring of *Eglifia*, but a Cheat paum'd upon them by thofe of *Aufonia*. In the next Place they made Application to the Prince of *Auromalia*, who had married the eldeft
Daughter

Daughter of the Emperor of *Grand.Infula*, and humbly intreated him to take Arms in Defence of his Lady's Title and that of her Sifter, after whom the Reverfion was in himfelf. The generous Prince comply'd with their Requeft, came with an Army to *Grand-Infula*, and had fo much Succefs, that the People in general revolted from *Idololatro*, who was forc'd to fly to *Ludovifia*, having fent his Emprefs with his couriterfeit Son *Don Diego Impoftore* thither before him.

This, *Sir*, is a fhort, but true Account of the Reafon why one half of our Grandfathers and Fathers Buckl'd on their Rufty Armour againft one another from time to time, and by the Way 'tis proper to obferve that in all thofe Turns the Rapparies of *Eglifia*, who ufurp'd the Title of *Loyalifts*, took part with the defpotical Emperors, againft the *Gerontes*, the Religion, the Laws and Liberties of *Grand-Infula*, fo long as they employ'd them to be the Inftruments of their Tyranny over their Fellow-Subjects, until fuch time as the Emperor *Idololatro* preferr'd the Rapparies of *Aufonia* before them: Whereas, on the other hand the *Philopatrians*, whom the other Party call'd by the opprobrious Name of *Levellers*, kept always true to the Conftitution, for which they were perfecuted by the Emperors and the Rapparies. *Idololatro* being thus forc'd from his Throne, the Prince of *Auromalia* fummon'd together an Affembly of the *Gerontes*, to confider what was fit to be done in fuch an extraordinary Conjuncture. In the mean time the Rapparies perceiving that things had gone further than they intended at firft, and being jealous that the Prince of *Auromalia*, who had been educated in the Religion of *Geneviaca*, and in the Politicks of

of *Ariſtocratia*, wou'd not continue to employ
them as they had been formerly, in the chief Poſts
of *Grand-Inſula*, and that he would endeavour
an Union of *Egliſia* and *Geneviaca*, they did all
that they cou'd to hinder his Advancement to the
Throne, and for that end reviv'd the Principles
they had formerly abandon'd, *viz.* That 'twas unlawful for them to reſiſt and dethrone their Emperor on any Pretence whatever; that therefore
he ought to be recall'd, and a Regency appointed
to take care of the Rights of *Egliſia*, that they
might be no more invaded by thoſe of *Auſonia*.
But the *Philopatrians* knowing very well that their
Deſign was only to ingroſs all the Power into
their own Hands again, by which the true Friends
of *Egliſia*, and thoſe of *Geneviaca* had ſmarted
ſo ſeverely, they carried it againſt them, and
after drawing up the ſeveral Articles of *Idolola-*
tro's Miſgovernment, they concluded with a
Reſolve, That his Throne was vacant, and that he
had loſt all Right to the Empire of *Grand-Inſula*.
After this, they ſet their Deliverer the Prince
of *Auromalia* and his Princeſs upon the Throne;
and in caſe of her Death without Iſſue, ſettled
the Reverſion on her Siſter and hers, after the
Death of the Prince of *Auromalia*, who was to
enjoy it during Life. The Rapparies of *Egliſia*
being thus diſappointed, they became ſworn Enemies to the Emperor *Auromalia* and his Princeſs,
as well as to the *Philopatrians*; they divided however into two Parties, one of whom made a Se-
paration both from *Egliſia* and the Empire, wou'd
not ſwear to the Emperor, and Empreſs, nor
have any Communion with thoſe of *Egliſia* who
ſubmitted to them. The other Party acted juſt
the Reverſe, for none were more forward to
com-

comply in both refpects than they. Some pleas'd
themfelves with a Diftinction that it was lawful
to comply with one who was Emperor *de facto*,
tho' he had no Title to the Throne *de jure* ; but
the Chief of 'em did it with a Defign to undermine the Empire and *Eglifia*, whilft others of a
lower Form did it that they might be capable of
advantagious Pofts. This created a terrible Faction both in *Eglifia* and the Empire, where the
Parties diftinguifhed themfelves by the Epithets
of *High* and *Low*; the former were join'd by the
Aufonian and Non-jurant Rapparies, and the
other by thofe of *Genevica*. The Divifion fpread
thro' the whole State, and got in among the
Gerontes, where the Rapparies gave the Emperor
all the Difturbance they cou'd in the Profecution of his juft War againft the Emperor of *Ludovifia*, who had openly efpous'd the Caufe of the
dethron'd *Idololatro*, with whom he had formerly
entred into a League to fubvert *Eglifia* and
Genevica, both in *Grand-Infula* ; and in *Continentia*, in Order to eftablifh the Emperor of *Ludovifia*'s defpotical Sway over the latter, and
Idololatro's over the former. To this end the
Emperor of *Ludovifia* fupply'd *Idololatro* with
Troops to recover the Empire of *Grand-Infula*,
but without Effect, all his Defigns being defeated by the fuperiour Genius and Courage of
the Emperor *Auromalia*. The Rapparies being
thus again difappointed, the chief of 'em enter'd into a Plot with the Emperor of *Ludovifia*,
and *Idololatro*, to murther the Emperor *Auromalia* and his Emprefs, and at the fame time to
invade *Grand-Infula* ; but this was difcover'd,
feveral of the Rapparies hang'd for it, *Auromalia*'s Fleet under the Conduct of a *Philopatrian*,

C   de-

defeated and burnt that of *Ludovisia*, and disappointed *Idololatro*'s Invasion. This prov'd a mortifying Blow to the Rapparies and *Ausonians*, oblig'd them to lay aside their violent Designs, and to have Recourse to Fraud and Cunning, for perceiving no Hopes of succeeding against *Auromalia* by Force, they attempted him by Treachery. To accomplish their Design they had Recourse to their old Topicks, by which they had got into the Favour of the tyrannical Emperor's, perswaded him that their Party was the only true Friends to the Emperor's Prerogative, and that the *Philopatrians* were Enemies to all Imperial Government, and Levellers by Principle. They had been join'd before in the meeting of the *Gerontes*, by several Apostate *Philopatrians*, who not receiving the Rewards they expected from the Emperor, were sowr'd in their Temper, and concurr'd with the Rapparies in every thing that might cross him. By this means their Party being strengthen'd, their Insinuations abovemention'd had the more Influence upon the Emperor, who thereupon put the Administration into their Hands, hoping by that means to bring them entirely to his Interest. One of these Apostate *Philopatrians*, who had a main Hand in making the Emperor uneasie, had formerly acquir'd a great Reputation for Learning, Parts, and Loyalty to the Constitution; but he was much disgusted with the Emperor, who, as he thought, did not only neglect his Merit, but had oppos'd his being one of the *Gerontes*, having some way or other been let in to his Character. This Gentleman from a topping *Philopatrian*, became a General of the Rapparies, who esteem'd him for his Intrigues, tho'

they

they were jealous of his Principles and Education.
To convince them therefore of his being fin-
cerely in their Interest, he drew several other
Philopatrians into the same Apostacy with himself,
and concurr'd in all the Measures of the Rapparies, outwardly at least ; for he was so dextrous,
that it seem'd always to be his principal Design
to secure himself a Retreat with either Party,
in Case he shou'd have Occasion for it, which
both being sensible of, they agreed as it were
by common Consent to give him the Name of
Epiboulius Astutus, so that his proper Name became an Apellative, to signify one that wou'd
circumvent another. In this State of Affairs
every thing went wrong in the Emperor's
hand, he being unhappily persuaded to disoblige his real Friends, when 'twas utterly impos-
sible for him to bring the Rapparies into the
true Interest of the Empire on which his own
was founded. The *Philopatrians* cou'd do little
else but sigh and pray for him, while he found
himself under a cruel Necessity to patch up a
Peace with the Emperor of *Ludovisia*, the best
way he cou'd, which was no wise pleasing, nor
advantagious, to his honest Subjects of *Grand-
Insula*. He saw his Mistake when too late, and
endeavoured to have rescu'd himself from the
Hands of his treacherous Enemies the Rapparies,
and to have put the Administration wholly into
the Hands of the *Philopatrians*, but Death prevented him.

'Tis necessary here to look back a little before we come to the Reign of his Successor
Heroina. The Rapparies being, as we said before, irreconcilable Enemies to the Emperor
Auromalia and his Empress, they did what they

cou'd

cou'd to create a Difference betwixt him, his
Emprefs, and *Heroina,* and endeavoured to perfwade the latter that fhe was injur'c by *Auromalia's* being prefer'd before her in the Entail of
the Crown: This occafion'd a Jealoufie, over
which we chufe to draw a Vail. This Rapparee
Plot was defeated however by the Goodnefs of
the Emprefs *Maria,* and the Wifdom of the
Emperor *Auromalia,* who cherifhed *Heroina*'s Son,
and fhew'd all the refpeft to her felf, which was
due to one who had the Legal Expectancy of fo
great a Reverfion as the Empire of *Grand-Infula.*
The Emprefs died in the mean time, Heaven
thinking her too great a Blefling to be continu'd among fo ungrateful a People. 'Twas
not long till fhe was followed by *Heroina*'s Son
into the Regions of Blifs, which prov'd two
fatal Strokes to the Security of the Peace and
Liberties of *Grand-Infula,* and were univerfally
regretted by the People; but amidft this publick
Grief the Rapparies indulg'd their malicious Refentments, and endeavour'd what they cou'd to
raife Animofities in *Heroina* againft the Emperor
Auromalia, as keeping her out of her Right;
this Difficulty was furmounted however by the
Prudence of the one, and Goodnefs of the
other, fo that the Rapparies fail'd in this Plot
as they had done in all the reft : Thus *Auromalia* continu'd in Poffeffion to the Day of his
Death with *Heroina*'s Confent, which feem'd to
have buried the flavifh Principle they call'd *Jus
hæreditarinm indefefibile,* and its Companion *Nulla
Refifentia,* without any fure and certain Hopes
of a Refurrection; and to prevent *Grand-Infula*'s
being haunted by the Ghofts of thofe trouble-
fome Criminals in time to come, and that it
fhou'd

ſhou'd not be in the Power of *Ludoviſia*, and *Don Diego Impoſtore*, to frighten the Nation by ſuch Apparitions any more; the Emperor *Auromalia* juſt before his Death procur'd a Law by the *Gerontes*, that after the Deceaſe of *Heroina* without Iſſue, the Reverſion of the Empire ſhou'd deſcend to the next Heir in the Faith of *Egliſia*, with the perpetual Excluſion of the neareſt in Blood that were of the ſame Opinion with the *Mufti* of *Auſonia*.

This the Rapparies did in all Converſation openly condemn as a curſed Legacy left the Nation by the Emperor *Auromalia*, but *Heroina* ſucceeding, according to the Laws made upon *Idololatro*'s Dethronement, they were not able to bring their Deſigns to bear for ſetting *Don Diego Impoſtore* upon the Throne. The next thing therefore they had Recourſe to was to load the Memory of *Auromalia* with all the Reproaches they cou'd, and they endeavour'd to poſſeſs the Minds of the People with an Opinion, that he had form'd a Deſign to ſet aſide the Succeſſion of *Heroina*, and to bring the Family of *Munlandia*, who were lineally deſcended from *Jago Vulpecius* immediately to the Throne. The Rapparies ſpread this Calumny with ſo much Induſtry that the *Amphyctiones*, the moſt eminent Part of the *Gerontes*, took it into Conſideration, appointed ſome of their own Number to examine *Auromalia*'s Papers, to ſee if there were any ſuch thing, and finding it to be a groundleſs Calumny, they declar'd, in Conjuction with *Heroina*, that it was falſe, villainous and ſcandalous, to the Diſhonour of the late Emperor's Memory, and to the Diſſervice of the preſent Empreſs; and order'd the Authors or Publiſhers of that

or

or such like Reports, to be prosecuted according to Law. This Design of the Rapparies being likewise defeated, they had Recourse again to their old Engine of suggesting the Empire to be in Danger by *Aristocratians*, the *Geneviacans* and *Eutacteglisians*, whom they represented to the Empress as *Levellers* and Enemies to her Prerogative. In this they had too much Success, which prevail'd upon the Empress to turn out the *Philopatrians*, and take the Rapparies into her Administration, in all which *Astutus Epiboulius* had the main hand, for Power and Riches he wanted, and must have 'em at any rate.

The Rapparies thought themselves now sure of every thing; they went on to asperse the Memory of *Auromalia* and all his Friends, ador'd the very Beast from which he receiv'd a Fall that hasten'd his Exit, and treated him as an Usurper, in Order to make void all the Laws that had been enacted during his Reign. There remained nothing for them to do, but to get an Assembly of the *Gerontes* of their own Stamp, in order to overturn every thing that had been done since the Dethronement of *Idololatro*, whose *Ausonian* and Rapparee Friends were so elevated with Hopes of Success, that one of 'em boldly dedicated a Book to the Empress and the *Gerontes*, wherein he asserted the Title of *Don Diego Impostore*, whom he call'd her Brother, and advis'd her to keep the Throne for him in Exclusion of the Line of *Mumlandia*. This pass'd not only without a Reproof, but the treasonable Author was rewarded. In the mean time the Rapparee *Gerontes* not thinking it safe to appear openly for *Impostore*, they were resolv'd for time to come, so to model the Senate, that

no *Geneviacan* or *Eutacteglisian* should hencefor-
ward be an Elector for it, admitted to it, or
to any Post of Power and Profit in the Empire
of *Grand Insula*, and to this end they propos'd
a Law for three Years successively, which was
as often rejected by the *Amphyctiones*, and the
whole Empire became so uneasie under this Rapparee Management, that the Empress thought
fit to change Hands again, to turn out most of
the Rapparies, and to take the *Philopatrians* into
the Administration. *Astutus Epiboulius* continu'd
however in his Post, and endeavour'd like a
Mole to undermine both the *Philopatrians*, and
the Constitution of *Grand-Insula*. There were
two great Men who stood in his Way, the one
call'd *Gazophilacius*, the other *Strategomacarius*,
because of their successful Care for the Nation,
whom the factious *Epiboulius* did all he cou'd
to get both of 'em turn'd out by the Interest
of *Alectia*, but without Effect, the Empress being
too sensible of the Merits of those two great Persons to listen to any such Advice. In the mean
time the *Amphictyones* being aware of *Epiboulius*'s
Artifice ; they enquir'd a little into his Conduct,
and finding there was reason to suspect that he had
an underhand Correspondence with the Emperor
of *Ludovisia*, and *Impostore* ; they found, upon Enquiry, that there was too good Ground for the
Suspicion, as appears by the Papers which they
order'd to be publish'd on that Head, and by an
extraordinary *Tendresse* which he discover'd for
a beautiful *Alopecia* that was employ'd as an
Emissary betwixt *Ludovisia*, and *Grand-Insula*, for
which she was taken up, but rescued by his Dex-
terity ; notwithstanding all this, *Epiboulius* found
means by *Alectia*, to screen himself from the Punishment

nifhment he deferv'd, and by *Colmanizing* one of his inconfiderable Grammatifta's, who kept a Correfpondence with *Ludovifia*, came cff without any other Lofs than that of his Poft.

'Tis very obfervable, that at the very Time while *Epiboulius* was endeavouring to undermine *Gazophilacius*, and *Strategomacarius*, the Emperor of *Ludovifia*, fent *Impoftore* with a Force to invade *Grand-Infula*, and to dethrone the Emprefs; which being taken Notice of by the ·*Amphyctiones*, they addrefs'd *Heroina* againft *Alectia*, who had been the principal Tool in the Hand of *Epiboulius*, to carry on his pernicious Defigns. Thefe Proceedings of the *Amphyctiones*, with the Zeal of the other *Gerontes* againft *Impoftore*, and the turning out of his Friends, made the intended Invafion of no effect; which once more difappointed the blooming Hopes of the Rapparies. They had fo much Intereft notwithftanding by means of *Alectia* and *Hauteglifia*, as to ward off the Punifhment which fo traiterous a Confpiracy deferv'd, and to preferve thofe from the Gallows, who were actually taken in Rebellion. This gave them time to recover their Breath, and to renew their Plots againft the Emprefs of *Grand-Infula*, and the Succeffion of the House of *Mumlandia*. Finding that all their forcible Attempts were difappointed, and that there was no Poffibility for them to fucceed by any other Way than poffeffing the People and the Emprefs with an Opinion that *Eglifia* was in Danger. *Epiboulius*, who from being a feemingly zealous *Geneviacan* and a *Philopatrian*, was now, become their fworn Enemy becaufe they had found him out, advis'd the Rapparies to fearch their *Gymnafia* and *Hauteglifia* for the moft daring and im-

and impudent Tongue-Pads to found an Alarm
thro' the Nation that the *Philopatrians* had a
Defign to dethrone the Emprefs, to overturn
Bafileia and *Eglifia*, and to fet up in their ftead
Arifocratia and *Geneviaca*, under the Protector-
fhip of *Strategomacarius*. The Party having thus
fitted themfelves according to *Epiboulius*'s Advice with *Hauteglifian* Firebrands to inflame the
Nation ; fome of 'em by means of *Alectia*, were
introduc'd to the Emprefs's Prefence, and in
her Hearing advanc'd the flavifh Doctrines of
Hauteglifia, in order to frighten *Heroina* with
the Ghofts of *Jus hereditarium indefefibile*, and
Nulla Refiftantia, of which by the Inchantments
abovemention'd they had procur'd a Refurrection,
in order, as they gave out, to refcue *Eglifia* from
Danger, tho' the Emprefs with her *Amphyctio-*
ones and *Gerontes*, had folemnly declared *Eglifia*
to be in no Danger, but in a very flourifhing
Condition ; and that thofe who fuggefted the
contrary were Enemies to the Emprefs, *Eglifia,*
and *Grand-Infula*. The Revival of thefe ground-
lefs Calumnies occafion'd feveral of the *Philo-*
patrians, and particularly thofe of *Eutacteglifia*
to write againft them, and confute them with
unanfwerable Arguments, which the *Hauteglifi-*
ans being fenfible of, and defpairing to maintain
their Caufe by Reafon, they betook themfelves
to Railing, reproach'd the *Philopatrians* from the
Prefs and Pulpit, and what they wanted in Lo-
gick made up with Billingfgate, wherein they
had the Affiftance of the *Aufonians*, and all the
Nonjurant Rapparies.

This new Method had a greater effect than
cou'd well have been imagin'd, upon the Minds
of a People who had been formerly noted, to

D   be

be more zealous than their Neighbours, for Religion and Liberty; but though the Operation
was fpeedy, 'twas not quick enough for the
Expectations of the Rapparies; for they faw
their Hopes were all like to be defeated by the
victorious Arms of the Emprefs, which under
the Conduct of *Strategomacarius* crown'd every
Campaign with new Victories, and the Conquefts of Towns and Provinces.

This infpir'd them with a Panick Fear, that
the Emperor of *Ludovifia* wou'd be reduc'd fo
low, as not to be able to fupport, and make good
the Pretenfions of their beloved *Impoftore*; therefore they made it their Bufinefs to ftop the
Progrefs of *Strategomacarius*'s Arms, by fuggefting
malicioufly to the Emprefs, that he aim'd at no
lefs than her Crown by the Intereft of the *Philopatrians*; that he prolong'd the War, on purpofe
to enrich himfelf and his Friends, who had the
Management of the publick Money; and that
his near Relation and chief Friend *Gazaphylacius*
mifapply'd the Treafure of *Grand-Infula*, ftarv'd
every Caufe but that of *Strategomacarius*, who,
together with himfelf laid up immenfe Sums, in
order to accomplifh their ambitious and treafo-
nable Purpofes. At the fame time they endeavoured to create Jealoufies in the Emprefs of
Strategomacarius's Lady, who for many Years had
been her Favourite and faithful Servant, and
labour'd with great Induftry to ruin her in the
good Opinion of the Emprefs. *Alectia*, whom
this Lady had introduc'd into the Emprefs's Service, upon a fatal Miftake of her Gratitude and
other Qualifications, was the Inftrument they
made ufe of to fupplant her Patronefs, by whofe
means fhe had arriv'd to a more than ordinary

Degree

Degree of the Emprefs's Favour. *Alectia* willing
to raife her felf at the expence of this Lady's
Reputation, tho' fhe ow'd her Bread to her,
did greedily imbibe, and exactly follow the Inftructions of *Epiboulius*, to ferve the Intereft of
Impoftore and the Rapparies ; or more proper-
ly fpeaking, to gratify his own Paffions, which
he always preferred to every thing elfe. By
this means the *Hauteglifians* came gradually to
grow in Favour with the Emprefs, and feem'd
very confident of being able to carry their Point;
but *Gazophylacius*'s Care and *Strategomacarius*'s
continu'd Succefs, ftill fpoiling their Meafures,
they confulted together on the beft Methods to
ftop his Progrefs, and cou'd think on none more
effectual than this, That the Emperor of *Ludovifia*
fhou'd fend Ambaffadors to the Court of *Septem
Choranea*, and propofe a Peace on feemingly reafonable Terms (but couch'd in fraudulent Expreffions) to the Emprefs and her Allies, while
they in the mean time wou'd endeavour to en-
cline her to accept his Propofals; and if the
Philopatrians oppos'd it, they wou'd improve the
Opportunity, to perfwade her that they did it
in Concert with the two great Men abovemention'd, on purpofe to fill their own Coffers, and
to ruin her Army by hazardous Battles, and
dangerous Sieges, that fhe might have no vete-
ran Troops to oppofe them, when their Defign
for feizing her Crown was brought to Maturity;
at the fame time they took Care to fpread thefe
malicious Suggeftions thro' all the Territories of
Grand-Infula, in order to poifon the Minds of
the People, and to inflame them with Rage
againft the *Philopatrians*, who had no other Defign in continuing the War, but that they might

dif-

difable the Emperor of *Ludovifia* from being in a Condition to purfue his Aim at univerfal Empire, and from forcing *Impoftore* upon themfelves, to the manifeft Overthrow of their Religion and Liberties. The Emperor of *Ludcvifia* fent his Ambaffadors to *Septem-choranea*, with Inftructions according to this Advice, on purpofe to render the Emprefs and her Allies fecure, and in order to gain time for retrieving the ill State of his own Affairs, his Country being vifited with Famine and contagious Diftempers at the fame time, when the Emprefs and her Allies were daily gaining ground upon him, had enter'd his Provinces, and laid feveral of em under Contribution. While the Emperor of *Ludovifia* chicand thus with the Confederates, *Epiboulius* and his trufty Friends in *Grand-Infula*, got *Mitrato Exoniaco* to make a *Hautegiifian* Difcourfe before the Emprefs, by which he ftruck at the very Foundation of her Government and Title, and advanc'd fuch Doctrines, as manifeftly tended to perfwade her that *Idololatro* was unjuftly dethron'd, and *Impoftore* as unjuftly kept out of his Right of Succeffion. The good Emprefs, who meafur'd other People's Sincerity by her own, not perceiving the Drift of that feditious Harangue, but conceiving that 'twas only defign'd to perfwade her Subjects to the general Duty of Obedience to her felf, was eafily prevail'd on to give her Authority for its Publication, which was improv'd by *Epiboulius*, and the reft of the Faction, to encourage all the Mandrits of *Hauteglifia* to proceed in the fame manner thro' the Nation, fince now they might be fure that the Emprefs was fully of their Sentiments. This provok'd an *Eutatieglifian* to anfwer

fwer *Mitrato*'s Difcourfe with very great Smart-
nefs and Judgment, wherein he laid open all the
Fallacies, and dangerous Confequences of his
Arguments with a great deal of Life and Spirit,
which renew'd the Paper and Pulpit War betwixt the *Philopatrians* and Rapparies with greater Fury than ever: The *Hauteglifians* had vifibly
the Difadvantage, but gain'd Ground notwithftanding upon the deluded People, by the Confidence they exprefs'd of the Emprefs's Favour.
Nothing could happen more opportunely for
reviving the drooping Spirits of the Emperor of
Ludovifia and his Subjects, or of *Impoftore* and his
Adherents; for that Emperor perceiving that the
Hauteglifians were fo fuccefsful in raifing Divifions in *Grand-Infula*, it embolden'd him to infift
upon unreafonable Terms of Peace, fo that he
wou'd by no means agree to reftore the Empire
of *Bætiea* to the Family of *Oftenrifhia*, from whom
he had ufurped it, in Favour of his Grandfon.
This occafion'd the breaking off of the Treaty,
which was improv'd by the Rapparies againft
the *Philopatrians*, as having proceeded from their
Intrigues to continue the War for their own Advantage. Yet every body elfe but the *Hautegli-*
fians were very well fatisfied, that the Emperor
of *Ludovifia* chicand, and that his Propofals did
not come any thing near the Terms, without
which the Emprefs and her *Gerontes* had again
and again declar'd they wou'd never make Peace
with *Ludovifia*.

In the mean Time *Strategomacarius*, whom the
Emprefs employ'd as Plenipotentiary for the
Treaty, as well as General to command her Armies, being provok'd with this *Ludovifian* Chica-
nery, he pufh'd on the War with Vigor, took
feveral

several of their strongest Towns, and defeated their Army in a bloody Battle, at a vast Disadvantage. The malicious Rapparies were so far from being put to the Blush by this Great Man's Sincerity, by his indefatigable Industry, and by exposing himself to all Dangers, that on the contrary they improved them to his Disadvantage, and because the Victory, tho' very glorious, was bloody. they charg'd him with having needlesly expos'd the Empress's Troops to unsurmountable Dangers; in order to ruin them, for the Purposes above-mention'd: However the Event has shew'd the *Ludovisians* to be so much dispirited by the great Loss they sustain'd in that Battle, and so terribly afraid of the superior Courage of *Strategomacarius* and his Troops, that they have never since offer'd to venture another Engagement with him. The *Hauteglisians* being more and more afraid, as indeed they had very good reason, that his Courage and Conduct, and the wise Management of the *Philopatrians* in the Empress's Service wou'd undo them, they renew'd their Attempts against them with greater Fury than ever, continu'd to instill Jealousies in the Mind of the Empress, and every where founded an Alarm thro' the Nation by their *Hauteglisian* Mandrits, That the Empress and *Eglisia* were in the utmost Danger by the *Philopatrians*, and the Ministry of their Principles. Among others, they pick'd out a *Hauteglisian* Priest, call'd *Don Enrico Maniaco*, a Fellow of superlative Impudence, to make a seditious Harangue in the Metropolis of *Grand-Insula*, before Senior *Stolido Outidano* the Consul, a sworn Friend to *Hauteglisia*, *Ausonia*, *Ludovisia*, and *Impostore*. This Consul gave *Maniaco* Authority to publish
his

his frantick Difcourfe under the Patronage of his Name, for to fay the Truth, a fitter Patron was not to be fouhd throughout *Grand-Infula*. This Harangue being an ill digefted piece of Rhapfody, collected out of all the Malicious Libels that had ever been Publifh'd againft the *Philopatrians*, *Eutacteglifians*, and *Geneviacans*, was induftrioufly handed all over the Empire by the *Hauteglifians*, on purpofe to raife a Rebellion againft the Emprefs, if fhe wou'd not turn out her *Philopatrian* Miniftry, and put Rapparees in their Place, by whofe Affiftance they might pave the way for bringing *Impoftore* to the Throne.

In the mean time the Succefs of *Strategomacarius* had fo far Humbled the Emperor of *Ludovifia*, as to make him beg leave once more to fend his Plenipotentiaries to *Septem choranca* to treat of a Peace in good earneft. The Rapparees being Mortally afraid that the ill pofture of that Tyrant's Affairs wou'd oblige him to confult his own Security, and to drop them and their beloved *Impoftore*, they fent him advice from time to time of the Succefs they had by Raifing Divifions in *Grand-Infula*, and therefore intreated him not to conclude a Peace too haftily, for they cou'd affure him, that by purfuing the Directions concerted betwixt his Court and that of *Impoftore*, they fhould be able to break the Meafures of the Confederacy, to leave his Grandfon in full Poffeffion of the Empire of *Bætica*, and inable him to fet *Impoftore* on the Throne, in fpight of all the *Philopatrians* could do to prevent it. This had the defign'd Effect, for the Emperor knowing that their own Security would oblige them to keep touch with him if they cou'd, he continu'd his Plenipotennipotentiaries in *Septem-choranea* to amuse the Empress and her Confederates, and to gain time to see whether the Rapparees, *Ausonians*, and *Hauteglisians* in *Grand-Insula*, would be able to perform their promise

The Campaign being over, and the *Gerontes* of *Grand-Insula* assembled, the *Philopatrians* were sensible that the *Hauteglisians* carry'd on the Interest of *Impostore*, by the Doctrine and Libels which they spread thro' *Grand-Insula*, and therefore they thought fit to call their furious *Antesignanus Enrico Maniaco* to an account for his Harangue, not that they thought the Man worth their Notice, but because they knew him to be imploy'd by the Faction of *Ludovisia* and *Impostore* to inflame the Minds of the People against the Government, there not being a *Hauteglisian Mandrit* in the Island of a more Prostitute Conscience, a Softer Brain, and a harder Forehead than himself; besides being a sworn Devoto to *Venus* and *Bacchus*. They knew that all the Non-resisting Ladies and *Hauteglisian* Rakes, esteem'd his Doctrine for the sake of his Person, as well as of his Principles, and endeavour'd to Propagate it all they cou'd.

Maniaco, when call'd before the *Gerontes*, was drop'd by his Patron Senior *Stolido*, who disown'd he had given him his Authority to Publish his Stygian Harange, which smell'd so strong of Brimstone, that every one, but those of the Faction, understood it to be the Composition of a Swarm of Locusts, that had been rais'd from the bottomless Pit, by the *Ausonian*, and *Hauteglisian* Inchantments, on purpose to infect *Grand-Insula* with a Spirit of Division and Fury.

Mighty

Mighty Endeavours were us'd to prevent *Ma-niaco*'s being brought to his Tryal, becaufe the *Hauteglifians* knew 'twould bring the Cenfure of the *Gerontes* upon the Doctrine they had advanc'd, in order to fet *Impoftore* on the Throne, who in Gratitude had promis'd to give them all the Pofts in the Empire, and to make *Hauteglifia* as Inde-pendant upon the Crown as her Mother *Aufonia*, and to reftore them all the Lands that had for-merly belong'd to the. Mufti and his Shavelings. But all their endeavours were to no purpofe, for neither their Threats nor their Promifes were regarded by the Majority of the *Gerontes*, who were ftanch *Philopatrians*. They proceeded there-fore to try *Maniaco* in a Solemn manner, for Li-belling the Memory of the Emperor *Auromalia*, for cafting Odious Reflections upon him, and thofe who joyn'd him in Refcuing *Grand-Infula* from the Tyranny of *Ludovifia*, and the Idolatry of *Aufonia*, and for blackening and condemning the means by which that Delivery, and the De-thronement of *Don Diego Idololatro* were effected. They charg'd him likewife with Libelling the Adminiftration of the Emprefs and her *Philopa-trian* Minifters, for accufing the Superior and Inferior *Paftors* of *Eutacteglifia*, as Falfe Brethren, and Enemies to the Emprefs, to God, to *Eglifia* and *Grand-Infula*, and for Seditioufly attacking the Liberty of Worfhip, which the Legiflature had granted to the *Geneviacans*, the better to unite all thofe who were of the fame Faith with *Eglifia*, and to ftrengthen the hands of the Em-prefs of *Grand-Infula*, againft the Violence and Intrigues of the Emperor of *Ludovifia* and *Im-poftore*. It being evident that *Maniaco* was prompted to do all this in order to raife a Re-

E   bellion,

bellion, the *Gerontes* went on with his Tryal.
The *Hauteglisians* were glad of the Opportunity,
tho' they dreaded the issue of the process, to raise
a ferment among the People, and therefore gave
out with the greatest Impudence, that the design of the *Philopatrians* to Ruin *Eglisia*, and to
pull down the Prerogative of the Empress, did
now plainly appear aboveboard, since the *Philopatrians* had the boldness to Attack *Enrico* for
maintaining those Doctrines, which were the
principal support of the Throne and *Eglisia*.
They assisted *Enrico*, and others, to Write and
Publish Libels against the *Gerontes*, and were
very liberal of their own and the *Ludovisian*
Money, to raise Mobbs, and interrupt the Legal
Proceedings against him. The *Hauteglisians* of
Impostore's Faction having always a parcel of the
late *Idololatro's* Officers, with others from *Ludovisia*, ready in Pay for such Emergencies, they
sent them out in disguise, with a hired Rabble, to
attend *Maniaco* to his Tryal, and to take all op-
portunities to raise Tumults in the Streets. A
Hauteglisian, who from an Usurer and a *Gram-
matist*, was become a Chevalier, furnish'd *Maniaco* with Coaches and Horses, to carry himself
and some other Rapparee Mandrits that were to
assist him, in great State to the Assembly of the
Gerontes, were *Manioco* behav'd himself with all the
Impudence that Wine, Women, Money, and the Secret Assurance of being brought off without Da-
mage cou'd Inspire into him, and was Huzza'd too
and fro from his Tryal by the Rascally Mobb
that was hir'd for Money, or procur'd by the
Interest of the *Ausonians* and *Hauteglisians*. Having proceeded thus for some time without Opposition, they were emboldned to go further, and
one

one Evening after they had attended *Maniaco*
back from his Tryal, they sent out their Mobb
under the Leaders abovemention'd to insult the
Gerontes as they went home from the Senate
Houfe, and to burn and pull down the Temples
of the *Geneviacans* and *Eutacteglifians*. Among
thofe who rais'd this Rebellious Mobb, the Clerk
of a Chevalier call'd *Anaideia*, who, tho' he be
fince advanc'd, is not yet rais'd fo high as his Merit, was one of the moft forward. They proceeded with great Fury, deftroy'd feveral of the
abovemention'd Temples, affaulted many of the
Gerontes in the Streets, and threatned to burn
their Houfes, which, together with the *Repofito-*
rium Del Banco, that fupports the Credit of
Grand-Infula, they intended to have Deftroy'd ;
but were happily prevented, chiefly by the Care
and Zeal of one of the *Amphyctiones*, a near Relation to *Strategomacarius*, and in a great Poft
under the Emprefs, who order'd a Party of her
Guards to difperfe the Mobb, which they did
with great Courage and Speed. This oppofition
foon quell'd the Courage of the *Hauteglifians*, who
found there was nothing to be done by Arms
while the *Philopatrians* had fo much Power in the
State : Therefore they forbore any more fuch exploits, tho' they took care not only to keep up, but
to increafe the ferment in the Minds of their deluded followers. When the *Gerontes* met next day,
they refolv'd on an Addrefs to the Emprefs to
make ufe of her Authority to prevent fuch Tumults
for time to come, and to iffue a Royal Proclamation, to fignify to the Subjects, that the *Aufo-*
nians, Non jurant *Hauteglifians*, and other Enemies to her Perfon and Government, had rais'd a
Rebellion to interrupt the Legal Proceedings of

the

the *Gerontes* againſt *Maniaco*, forbidding any
Perſons on Severe Penalties to do the like in time
to come, and offering a Reward to thoſe, who ſhould
diſcover the fomenters of the late Rebellion.
The *Hautegliſians* in the Aſſembly, beirg ſecretly
encourag'd by *Epiboulius* and the Chevalier *Anaideia* abovemention'd, *&c.* They had the Bold-
neſs to oppoſe this Addreſs, and thought to have
thrown it out, by getting the *Ariſtocrateians* in-
ſerted in it, as incouragers of the Rebellion; but
'twas carried againſt them, and their amendment
rejected with ſcorn, becauſe the *Philopatrians* are
for no ſuch form of Government, tho' it be Ma-
liciouſly objected againſt them.

A Proclamation was accordingly Publiſh'd,
which, with raiſing the Military Force of the
Metropolis, put an end to the like Violent attempts there, and the *Gerontes* went on with the
Tryal of *Maniaco*. But tho' the Rapparees receiv'd this Mortifying Check, they did not loſe
Courage, being ſupported under-hand by *Epiboulius, Alettia, &c.* ſo that they went on to raiſe
the like Tumults in ſeveral Places of *Grand-Inſula*,
where the *Auſonians* and *Hautegliſians* declar'd
boldly againſt the Tryal of *Maniaco*; Cry'd him
up as the Champion of *Egliſia*, and their Leaders
in the Country had Letters from thoſe in the
Metropolis, aſſuring them that they might do
it without any Danger, and ſhou'd be juſtified in
it. Theſe Things, with the Seditious Harangues
of the *Hautegliſian Mandrits*, who perſwaded
their Ignorant Auditors, that *Hautegliſia* and
Baſileia were in danger, increaſ'd the fury of the
Rabble, ſo that every Poſt brought News from
the Country of the Outrages and Inſults they
committed upon the *Philopatrians*: They Poor
People

People did not expect this, and were no wise provided against it, but cou'd easily have quell'd them had they not thought themselves secure under the Protection of the Law, and been resolv'd to shew better example than to Usurp any Part of the Executive Power. The *Hauteglisians* knew how to improve this different Conduct of the Two Parties to their own Advantage. *Epiboulius* took care by, means of *Alectia*, to represent the outrages of his *Hauteglesian* Friends in Town and Country as the effect of their Courage and Numbers, and the Peaceable behaviour of the *Philopatrians*, as that of their Weakness and Fear. This he did in order to possess the Empress with an Opinion that 'twas not safe for her to disoblige the former for the sake of the latter ; and thus left his Insinuations to Operate like some sort of Poisons, which tho' they be slow are sure.

In the mean time the *Philopatrians* trusting to the Goodness of their Cause, the Uprightness of the Empress, and their own Sincerity, went on with the Tryal of *Maniaco*, allow'd him to make all the defence he cou'd, and having fully prov'd their Charge, permitted him to speak for himself, which he did with such a mixture of Impudence, Falshood and Perjury, as could proceed from the Mouth of none but an Infernal Locust ; he foreswore the Facts which were fully prov'd from his own Writings to be true ; Pretended a Mighty Zeal for the Empress, tho' he had been known to Condemn her as an Usurpress ; deny'd that such and such Articles were pointed against her Ministry, tho' he had own'd the contrary to several who hear'd him ; he foreswore his being in *Impostore*'s Interest, tho' he had been frequently
known

known to have drunk his Health; he deny'd
that he reflected on *Auromalia*, tho' he had openly
wish'd he might be tore to Pieces; he would not
own that he reflected on the superior Pastors of
Eglisia, tho' he condemn'd them in his Writings
as *false Brethren*, because they did not anathema-
tize the *Geneviacans*; and with the like Assurance
he forswore his condemning the Liberty granted
to them by Law, tho' he had expresly asserted
the Legislative Power to deserve a double Load
of Damnation for having granted it.

This Behaviour of *Maniaco*, as it convinc'd
the *Philopatrians* that he was the most worthless
and impudent Tool ever made use of by a Party, it rais'd him in the esteem of the Rapparies
and *Ausonians* as one of the most useful Instru-
ments that *Grand-Insula* cou'd furnish for the
Works of Darkness they had in hand. Therefore in Order to save him if possible from the
Punishment due to his Crimes, they rais'd many
trifling Objections in Point of Law against his
Trial; besides which they made use both of
Promises and Threats to influence the *Amphyctiones* in passing their Sentence upon him.

They wou'd willingly have had him acquitted,
but that proving in vain, they obtain'd so much
Interest by means of *Epiboulius* and *Alectia*, as
prevail'd with many of the *Amphyctiones* who
cou'd not acquit him, to sollicit for a moderate
Sentence against him. Upon this the Rapparees
triumph'd all over the Kingdom, ascrib'd it to
the Fear and Weakness of the *Philopatrians*, and
to their own Number, Strength and Interest;
by which the *Hauteglisian* Mandrits, and *Impostore*'s Faction, became more insolent than ever.
The *Philopatrians* thinking they had done enough
by

by this Trial and Cenfure, to prevent the like Infults upon the Conftitution in time to come, and perhaps being deluded by their too great Confidence in the Goodnefs of their Caufe, and the Promifes of thofe who were chiefly concern'd to fupport it, they neglected to take fuch Precautions as were neceffary to clear *Eglifia*, the *Gymnafia*, and the Pofts of *Grand-Infula* from *Impoftore*'s Friends, and to enact fuch pofitive Laws; with proportionable Penalties, as might deter the *Hauteglifians* from the like feditious Practices. Thus after finifhing the Bufinefs that remain'd for the Support of the War, the Affembly of the *Gerontes* was difmifs'd, and thank'd by the Emprefs for their Zeal and Affection, and particularly for their Proceedings againft *Maniaco*, which fhe approv'd as neceffary. The *Hauteglifians* were not content with their Succefs in bringing off *Maniaco* fo eafily, becaufe they knew, that tho' the Penalty was light, the Cenfure lay heavy upon their Conduct and Principles; therefore they refolv'd at any rate to eafe themfelves of that intolerable Grievance, and to revive thofe flavifh Principles, which were fo neceffary to introduce *Impoftore* with *Ludovifian* Politicks, and the *Aufonian* Religion, and at the fame time to bury the *Gerontes* with as much unjuft Reproach as they had done their beloved Doctrine with juft Contempt. In order to prepare *Heroina* for this, they had before hand engag'd the Mitrato's and Mandrits of *Hauteglifia*, and all their Adherents and Rapparies to addrefs *Heroina* with mighty Proteftations of Loyalty to her Perfon and Government, and at the fame time to affert their lately condemn'd Principles as the Doctrine of *Eglifia* and the Apoftles,

ftles, and to be the fundamental Laws of *Grand-Infula*, without which the Emprefs and her Monarchy could not be fafe. They had Initructions likewife from *Epiboulius*, who was always as great a Mafter at double *Entendres* as Practices, to reflect upon the *Gerontes* and *Philopatrians*, as being in a Plot to overturn *Eglifia* and *Bafileia*, of which they alledged their condemning the above-mention'd Principles was an evident Proof. They were further inftructed to prevent the Difcovery of their Defign by the People of *Grand-Infula*, to pretend an extraordinary Zeal for the Succeffion of the Houfe of *Muralandia*, but to keep their Intereft with *Impoftore*; they were to declare in the fame Breath for Non-refiftance and Hereditary Right: That they might gull *Eglifia*, they were taught to profefs an inviolable Zeal for her Legal Eftablifhment, and an utter Averfion for all Schifmaticks; and that they might not feem to revile the Legifla-ture, for the Indulgence granted by Law, they were enjoin'd to exprefs a tendernefs for Conf-cences truly fcrupulous. The Method of ad-dreffing being thus concerted by *Epiboulius*, and the other Leaders of the *Hauteglifians*, Models of 'em were difpatch'd to the Rapparee Man-drits and others thro' all the Provinces of *Grand-Infula*.

The next thing to be done was to find out a proper Perfon to break the Way, and the *Gerontes* were no fooner difmis'd, but *Don Scolido* the Conful undertook that Province, and with a Parcel of Rapparies under his Influence, pre-fented the firft Samplar of this Nature to the Emprefs: He found eafie Admittance by the In-tereft of *Epiboulius* and *Alectia*, and becaufe of
the

the Dignity of the Metropolis he reprefented. But the Emprefs not feeming at firft to relifh that fort of Compliment, becaufe of the Dangerous Confequences that might attend them if call'd in queftion by the *Gerontes*, as others of the like Nature had formerly been; *Epiboulius* and his Friends, thought it proper, for giving them the more Authority, to bring fome Rapparees of diftinction into great Offices about the Emprefs who might introduce them ; for the *Philopatrian* Minifters, difcountenanc'd all thofe Applications, becaufe they ftruck at the Conftition, reflected on the Legiflature, and were inconfiftent with that Approbation, which the Emprefs had publickly given to the Proceedings of the *Gerontes* againft *Maniaco*. To this end they brought into the Emprelfes Service *Hegemonius Verfatilis*, an *Aufonian* by Education, but had afterwards turn'd *Eglifian*, and profeffing himfelf to be a Zealous *Philopatrian*, fell in with thofe who were for Dethroning *Idololatro*, and Advancing *Auromolia*. *Hegemonius* being a Patrician of an ncient Family, and having acquir'd Reputation by his Parts and early appearance againft the *Ludovifian* Politicks and *Aufonian* Religion, he did in a little time obtain a very great Intereft in *Auromalia*'s Favour. and was look'd upon to be one of the Chief of the *Philopatrians* ; but being Difgufted fome way or other, he foon return'd to his Changeable Humour, and tho' in a Place of the higheft Truft under *Auromalia*, entred into a Confpiracy, with others, to Dethrone him, and conceal'd from him a Plot, which feveral *Aufonian*, and *Houteglifian* Affaffins had ingag'd in to Murther him. This being dilcover'd, and *Hegemonius* juftly fufpected, he retired, on pretence of his Health, to *Ludovifia* ; where he

F   had

had a Conference with that Emperor about Refto-
ring *Impoftore*, and the Religion of *Aufonia*; which,
to fay the Truth, was much better Accommodated
to his way of Living, than the Pure and Undefil'd
Religion of *Eglhfia*; but matters not being then
Ripe, *Hegemonius* Travell'd further to *Aufonia*,
where he was eafily reconcil'd to his old way of
Devotion; and to rivet him in it, the *Mandrits* of
Aufonia brought him Acquainted with *Donna
Porneia*, who foon forc'd him to Honour her with
the Title of *Hegemonia*. Sometime after *Aurotna-
lias*'s Death, thefe Two Perfons Arriv'd in *Arand-
Infula*, fully inftructed to carry on the defigns
of *Ludovifia*, and *Impoftore*, and being planted a-
bout the Emprefs by means of the *Hauteglifians*.
Hegemonius was judg'd the propereft Perfon to
introduce, and give Authority to that fort of
Addreffes, which afterwards grew fo much in
Vogue. With him the *Hauteglifians* join'd one
of their own Bigots, *Sunemporus Deifidamenius*, as a
fit Second; thefe Two, by the help of *Arcbimitrato
Borcius*, who had a great fway with the Emprefs
in matters relating to the other World, labour'd
hard to prepare her for what was to follow. The
next Perfon the *Hauteglifians* brought to act his
part, was Young *Hegemonius Porneiopoticos*, who
prefented the Second Compliment of that Nature, and behav'd himfelf with fuch Infolence,
as plainly enough difcover'd he was fure of being
well feconded; and thus the Humour of Ad-
dreffing went on. The *Philopatrians* were furpriz'd
with this unexpected, and Impudent way of pro-
ceeding, and endeavour'd to counter-act the Rapparies, by Applications of a contrary Nature,
wherein they had fo vifible an Advantage both as
to Truth, and Superiority of Genius, that the
Hau-

Hauteglifians found it neceffary by Artifice to put
a Stop to their Progrefs. The *Philopatrians* were
unhappily betray'd into this Negleft by fraudulent Suggeftions and Promifes, and by their
Confidence in *Heroina*'s being Proof againft the
Craft of her and their own Enemies.

The Rapparies, who had all things prepar'd
beforehand, improv'd this Negleft of the *Philopatrians* to their own Advantage, and doubling
their Diligence, did, by Threats, Flattery and
Money, procure fuch a Multitude of Addreffes
on their Side, as made the Emprefs believe that
the far greater Part of her Subjeфts of *Grand-Infula* were of their Mind; the *Hauteglifians* having alfo by the Affiftance of *Epiboulius* and
Alectia, and the crafty Infinuation of the *Aufonian Hegemonia*, perfwaded *Heroina* that they
were the only true Subjeфts, and the *Philopatrians* her Enemies ; they were refolv'd to ftrike
home, and to put the Emprefs upon a Change
of her *Eutacteglifian* Miniftry. This being a
Matter of Difficulty, becaufe the Emprefs had
fufficient experience of their Fidelity and Ability, the Rapparies met with fome Obftruфions,
which hinder'd the Projeфt from being put in
execution fo foon as they defir'd ; for thefe Diforders in *Grand-Infula* having put the Emperor
of *Ludovifia* upon breaking off his Treaties with
the Emprefs and her Confederates once more,
Heroina's Allies took the Alarm at it, reprefented to the Emprefs the Danger which thofe
Chadges might bring to the common Caufe,
and the Incouragement which they would give
to the Tyrant of *Ludovifia*, his Grandfon the
Ufurper of *Bætica*, and her own Capital Enemy
Impoftore : This put the Emprefs to a ftand for
                                                    fome

some time and wou'd have put a final Stop to
those intended Changes, had she been Mistress
of her self, and not betray'd into the Hands
of her Enemies, by *Epiboulius*, *Alectia*, and *Hegemonia*. The *Hauteglisians* being sensible that
the Miscarriage of this Design would ruin their
Affairs, they took all the Methods they cou'd
possibly think on to prevent it, and prevail'd
with the Empress first to turn out of her Service an eminent *Philopatrian*, a near Relation to
Strategomacarius, and one to whose Zeal the sup-
pressing of the Rebellion rais'd in Favour of
Maniaco, was principally owing. This Change
did very much alarm the *Philopatrians*, and gave
such a Blow to the Credit of *Grand-Insula*, as it
has not since been able to recover.

The Empress's Allies were likewise so much
concern'd at it, that they renew'd their Applications against those Proceedings, and in very
pressing Terms remonstrated the Danger of 'em.
Heroina being mov'd with this, and with the
Fall of the Nations Credit, was pleas'd graci-
ously to promise, both to her Allies, and to several of the chief Citizens of her Metropolis, That
there shou'd be no more Changes, and that she
wou'd continue the same *Gerontes*. This renew'd
the Confidence of the *Philopatrians*, who knew
the good Temper, and Sincerity of the Empress;
but alas! the good Lady was not so much Mistress of her self, as she reckon'd ; for *Epiboulius*
and his Friends knowing they must be ruin'd
for having gone so far, if they did not go further,
push'd on their Designs with the utmost Fury,
and by means of *Alectia* and *Hegemonia*, prevail'd
on the Empress to forget her Promises; incens'd
her against her Allies as meddling with what
they

they had nothing to do, and perſwaded her to turn out *Gazophilacius Synedrio Proeſtos, Archigrammatiſta,* and the reſt of the *Philopatrians* that ſtood in the way of *Impoſtore,* and his Supporter the Emperor of *Ludoviſia.* The principal Argument the *Hauteglifians* made uſe of to bring the Empreſs into thoſe Meaſures, was to poſſeſs her with an Opinion, That all the Subjects of *Grand·Inſula,* or at leaſt, the far greateſt Part of 'em, were of their Side, and that ſhe cou'd not be ſafe except ſhe concurr'd with them; and in Order to fix her in this Opinion, they not only went on with their Addreſſes as abovemention'd, but ſent *Maniaco* thro' a great Part of the Country, where the Rapparies, *Auſonians,* and *Hauteglifian* Mandrits were before-hand prepared to give him a magnificent Reception, and to attend him in a tumultuous Manner from one Place to another, in Order to ſtrike Terror into the *Philopatrians,* and to poſſeſs both Court and Country with a mighty Opinion of the Intereſt and Power of *Hauteglifia.* But that inſolent Mandrit behaving himſelf in ſuch a manner, as made both his Cauſe and Perſon to ſtink in the Noſtrils of thinking Men, they thought fit to recall him, left his Impudence ſhou'd do them more Hurt than Good; and after he had finiſh'd his Parade, they ſent their *Marius Hegemonious Porneius* into other Parts of the Country, to finiſh what *Maniaco* had begun.

The *Hauteglifians* having thus prepar'd Matters, and got the far greateſt Part of the Officers who return the Members of the *Grand Synedrium,* of their own Nomination, and having likewiſe prepar'd a great number of the Electors by Bribes, Debauches, and other diſhonourable Methods, they

pro-

procur'd the old Synedrium to be diffolv'd, and a
new one to be call'd. In this they had a mighty
Advantage of the *Philopatrians*, who relying on
Heroina's Promiſes, and her Knowledge of her own
true Intereſt, were not equally provided for ſuch
a Turn : Beſides *Epiboulius*, according to his uſual
manner, had chicand with them a conſiderable
Time, and pretending to accommodate Matters,
and only to demand a redreſſing of Grievances,
he deluded not a few of the unthinking *Philopatrians* into his Meaſures; whereas, on the
other hand, the *Hauteglifians* being let into the
Secret, doubld their Diligence, took all their
Precautions in Time, brought over great Numbers of the Electors by their Rapparee Mandrits,
and hir'd Raſcally Mobbs under the Conduct of
Impoſtore's and the Emperor of *Ludoviſta*'s Officers in Diſguiſe, to inſult the *Philopatrian* Candidates and their Adherents, to threaten their
Lives, and to fill the Nation with Tumults.
  In the mean time, when all theſe Meaſures
were taking to carry on the Intereſt of *Impoſtore*
in *Grand-Inſula*, *Epiboulius*, in order to put a
further Cheat upon the Nation, adviſ'd the
ſending a *Philopatrian* Apoſtate to the Court of
Mumlandia, to make them and the Nation believe
that no Prejudice was intended to their Succeſſion;
that the Rapparies were their firmeſt Friends,
and the *Philopatrians* their ſecret Enemies, being
rather for *Ariſtocratcia* or *Impoſtore*, than for their
Family. The Succeſs of this Meſſage appears by
the Event not to have been ſuch with that wiſe
Prince as the *Hauteglifians* thought it wou'd; ſo
that now all their former Pretences of calling
him over to command the Troops of *Grand-
Inſula*, or to give him ſome conſiderable Poſt in
the

the Empress's Dominions are dropp'd, and the
Rapparees are visibly pursuing another Game :
For having by the Methods above-mention'd procur'd a *Hauteglisian* and *Ausonian* Ministry, and
most of the *Gerontes* to be chosen out of the Rapparies, and *Impostore*'s known Friends, they seem
now ready to throw off the Disguise. This is
much more visible in *Albania*, where *Epibolita*
having, by means of a late Affinity, obtain'd a
great Interest among the Friends of *Ludovisia*
Impostore, he has discover'd the Falshood of his
Pretences, by getting the far greater Part of
the *Amphyctiones* from thence to be return'd
from among *Impostore*'s known Adherents. Every thing being thus concerted for advancing
that Interest, the *Ausonians* and *Ludovisians* are
big with Expectations of having all things go
to their Minds, and some of them have been
so free to their Confidents of late, as to make
their Boasts, That all things are concerted for
setting *Impostore* upon the Throne, that they
have Men Regimented on Purpose thro' *Grand-
Insula*, who are ready at a Call, and have their
Office and Places of Rendezvous appointed.
They say that having now the Mobb on their
Side, they will rise on a sudden upon a Pretence
of obtaining a further Security for *Eglisia*, to
have the Laws which indulge the Schismaticks,
repeal'd ; the *Geneviacans* of *Albania* overturn'd ;
and being once got together, will, by Night, cut
off the chief of the *Philopatrians*, of whose Persons
and Habitations they have distinct Accounts :
Upon this *Impostore* is to appear, will declare
himself a *Hauteglisian*, and by that means ascend
the Throne with the unanimous Consent of the
Rapparies. To accomplish this bloody and traiterous

terous Defign, they have brought over Multitudes of Cutthroats from *Potratonia,* with a fui-
table Proportion of Officers from *Ludovifia* ; fo
that with the *Aufonian* and *Hauteglifian* Mobb they
have lifted, the appearance of the *Ludovifian*
Fleet upon our Coaft, and fetting the Metropolis of *Grand-Infula* on Fire, they make no Doubt
to fucceed in the Enterprize ; and by effecting
an Union betwixt *Hauteglifia* and *Aufonia,* to
which the Rapparies are fo much enclin'd, they
conclude they fhall be able to fecure their Intereft for all time to come. This, *Sir,* is like
to be the Refult of the happy Change which
Epiboulius. Aleÿia, with *Hegemonius* and his Mate,
have brought about among us. God preferve
the Emprefs, *Grand-Infula.* and the Family of
Mumlandia, from thofe Antichriftian Defigns.

I am S I R, yours.

P. S. By what's faid above, you may eafily
judge whether *Grand-Infula* was more happy
under the the Quinquinvirate of the *Philopatri-*
ans, than 'tis like to be under the Triumvirate
and Tritheleiarchat of the Rapparies.

Hæc quota pars Scelerum qua cuftos Gallicus urbis
Ufq; a Lucifero donex Lex occidat audet.
                                                   Juvenal.

F I N I S.

The History
of the Proceedings
of the
Mandarins and Proatins
of the
Britomartian Empire

Anonymous

Bibliographical note:

This facsimile has been made from a copy in the Beinecke Library of Yale University (British Tracts 1712 H62)

THE
HISTORY
OF THE
PROCEEDINGS
OF THE

M AND *A* R *I N S* and *P* RO *ATINS*

OF THE

Britomartian Empire

AT THEIR

Laſt General Diet, with the Characters of the Chief Members.

———Captique dolis, donisque coacti,
Quos neque Tydides, nec Lariſſæus Achilles,
Non Anni domuere decem, non mille Carinæ.
Virg. Æn. 2.

LONDON:

Printed for the Bookſellers of *London* and *Weſt-*
minſter. 1712.   [Price 1*s*.]

THE
HISTORY
OF THE
PROCEEDINGS
OF THE
Mandarins and *Proatins*, &c.

IN the Infancy of the World, when Superstition was introduc'd by the Priesthood, to bring People under an implicite Obedience to its Arbitrary Dictates, and Bigotry was thought necessary for the Establishment of an absolute and unlimited Dominion, it was with the Empire of *Britomartia* as with other States; and those that Administer'd in holy Matters, (according to the Language of the Country call'd *Sacristo*'s) took upon them to prescribe Rules to Princes, and exact the Performance of their Injunctions from Crown'd Heads. This the Empress *Palatina* had prudently observ'd to be a great Diminution of Her Sovereign Authority : And in some time after Her Advancement to the Throne, (in the Room of the Deceas'd *Aurantia*) by the means of some faithful Councellors, who foresaw the Evil Consequences of it, Extri-

cated

cated herself out of the tame Submission her
former Credulity had made Her shew to
their Pious and Religious Frauds. From
thence-forward, She grew into the Highest
Reputation with all the *Potentates* of the
Earth, and Her Arms wheresoever they
were order'd to subdue and Conquer execu-
ted Her Commands. In a Word, She was
the Terror of Her Enemies, and the Delight
of Her Friends, and there was not a Prince
in the whole Univerfe that did not either
Court her Alliance, or dread to enter into
any thing like a Confederacy againft Her.
Sea and Land continued to furnifh her with
occasions of frefh Triumphs, and repeated
Victories, made appear the Wifdom of the
Adminiftration at Home, and the well concerted Meafures that were taken Abroad.
So that all Things occurr'd to the Increafe
of Her Glory, and fcarce any Accident of
Moment fell out, which did not Contribute
to the Honour of Her and Her People. But
as in all Governments, there are thofe that
malign at Exalted Merit, and bear Ill Will
to others Advancement; fo it happen'd a-
mong thofe that were Ambitious of Court
Preferment, that feveral Disbanded Minifters of State in Conjunction with the Priefts
who were for hurrying *Palatina* into Violent
Meafures againft all Religions but their own,
fo work'd themfelves into a Belief with the
Commonalty, that the National Worfhip
was

was in Danger from Her Imperial Majefty's Indulgence to fcrupulous Confciences, and the Exorbitant Power, which was pretended to be exercifed by thofe who were at the Helm of Government immediately under Her, that She not only gave into the Schemes of Her Domeftick Enemies by Difplacing Her beft Friends, but Affented to the defires of the Majority of her People, who were drawn into thofe Meafures by the Artifices above mention'd, in calling a new Diet of the Empire, and Iffuing out Edicts for their being conven'd together about *Arduous*, and Important Affairs.

It is not to be doubted, but the Choice of *New* Deputies was anfwerable to their Wifhes, who had prevail'd for the Difmiffion of the *Old*, and fince their Authority, who had before Officiated in the Chief Pofts and Dignities was funk to nothing, it is but reafonable to conclude, that thofe who were Invefted with them had a mighty Superiority; Becaufe where the Prey is to be found, there Affemble the *Ravens*, and Men of Voracious Appetites cannot but know, there is no Satiety to be expected from Tables that are ftripp'd of their wonted Delicacies.

Therefore after Elections had been carried in all the Provinces and Diftricts of the Empire, to the fatisfaction of thofe that influenc'd them from above, and it was apparent the Court had carried their Point

by

by a great Majority ; Both Orders and Degrees of Men in this Illuftrious Diet, met it
as had been accuftomed, in the *Pretorian-
Hall*, to Confult about the Neceffities of the
State, (which was the chief Motive of there
being called together) and the Welfare and
Advantage of the People.

The firft of thefe Two Eftates were the
Mandarines, or the *Noblefs* of the Empire,
whofe high Employment was to fit as Supreme Judges in Matters of Law ; a Court
of Judicature, from which there was no
Appeal, to give Advice to the Sovereign in
Cafes of Emergence, and to Redrefs the
Grievances of fuch as apply'd to them in
matters of Injury or Oppreffion. They fate
likewife as a Ballance of Power between
the Prerogatives of the Crown, and the
Rights and Immunities of the Subject, and
nothing could pafs into a *Decreto*, whether
it related to Aids and Supplyes of Money in
Times of War, or other Cafualties, to the
Punifhment of Offenders, whofe Crimes
were of an extraordinary Nature, and feemingly above the Cognizance of Inferior
Courts, or to the Confirmation, or Abrogati-
on of Privileges of Bodies Corporate, or private Perfons, without their Concurrence.

The Second Eftate confifted of the Weal-
thier and Wifer part of the Commonalty,
who being felected out from the whole *Populace*, were fent as Deputies to reprefent
the

the feveral Cities, Towns and Provinces, under the Empreffes Dominion, (whereas, thofe before Named were each of them, and feverally their own Reprefentatives) and thefe were called the *Proatins.* They fate in the *Pretorian-Hall* as the Grand Inqueft of the Empire, had the fole Right of raifing extraordinary Subfidies, and the Liberty of preparing and Promulging fuch Laws, as feem'd moft Conducive to the Good and Tranquillity of the Empire, and the Advantage of thofe that chofe them. It alfo belong'd to them, to Infpect the Management of the *Fifcalio,* and other Publick Offices, to enquire into Abufes that had crep'd into the Adminiftration, and to make Obfervations upon fuch Things as fell more immediately under their Notice, relating to Complaints of Corrupt Practices, or Reprefentations to theThrone,when theFunds they had given fell fhort of fupplying theNeceffities of the State,by the means of the Perfons in whofe Hands they were intrufted.

The *Reader* being thus appriz'd of what was Incumbent upon each Order of Men, that Compos'd this Auguft Affembly, is to be told in the next Place, that it was the Prerogative of the Imperial Dignity, either to give a Sanction to fuch Laws as had been mutually agreed to, between thefe Two Eftates, from whence they were called *Decreto's,* or elfe, to reject them, by a Refufal

A 4   fufal

fufal of its Affent, which made them altogether invalid, and of no Authority or Force.
It was cuftomary alfo at the Beginning of
every *Seffion*, for fo their Meeting was call'd,
for Him, or Her, who was Invefted with
the Sovereignty, to lay before them the
Reafons of their being thus Affembled,
which was at this Time to find out neceffary Ways and means for carrying on a War,
which had been Honourably begun, and
Succefsfully continued againft the Tyrannical Encroachments of a Perfidious Prince,
that aim'd at nothing lefs than Univerfal
Monarchy. Wherefore the Emprefs *Palatina* having fet before Them, " the Confi-
" dence She had in the Love and Duty of
" Her Subjects, by difmiffing the laft *Diet*
" and Old Counfellors, and in fupplying
" their Places with the new Deputies and
" Miniftry, lamented the heavy Debts
" which every Branch of the Revenue was
" charg'd with, afk'd Supplies from the *Pro-
" atins* (whofe fole Bufinefs it was to raife
" them) affur'd them of Her readinefs to
" comply with any Meafures, that fhould
" be taken to prevent any Incumbrances for
" the future, and told them She expected
" their Concurrence in all things, that fhould
" Conduce to the further Eftablifhment and
" Security of the National Worfhip, the
" Intereft of their Country, and the Ad-
" vancement of Her Honour, She laid Her
Commands

Commands upon the *Proatins* to chuſe an
Oratorio. and ſo left what She had ſaid to
their reipective Conſiderations.

Now this *Oratorio*, was to be a Perſon
well Veſ'd in the Conſtitution of the Empire, of a diſcerning Judgment, and of Un-
common Abilities, to carry him through
the Duties of ſo Important a Truſt. His
Office was to propoſe any Motion made by
any Member that was thought to be Bene-.
ficial to the Publick, to lay Petitions before
them, that Sued either for the Redreſs of
Old Grievances, or requeſted the Conceſſion
of new Previleges, and to have Acceſs to
the Throne upon all Occaſions, by way of
Remonſtrance againſt whatſoeverEncroach-
ments or Invaſions ſhould be made upon
the Liberties of the Subject. But as theſe
Gentlemen were for the greateſt Part, rather choſen to ſerve a particular Set of Men,
than the Intereſt of their Country ; ſo they
did not Elect a Perſon to this High Dignity, altogether from the Conſideration of
the foregoing Character, but had other
Motives in View, which were of great
Weight with them, to fix upon a Man that
ſhould readily give into the Meaſures that
had been before Concerted. They knew
that *Don Wilhelmino* was an Irreconcileable
Enemy, to ſuch as were againſt precipitate
and *dangerous Experiments* ; they put the
greateſt Confidence immaginable his Zeal
for,

for, and *Bigotry* to, the *Montalti*'s Principles
which breath'd nothing but Perfecution,
and they had made Tryal upon feveral Occafions of his unalterable Refolution to be
ftill complaining without a Caufe, and always pufhing at Endeavours to remedy
Grievances that never were in Being.
Wherefore they pitch'd upon Him to prefide in their Seffion, after *Don Thomafio*, a
Deputy of the Equeftrian-Rank had Har-
rangued Him into that Poft, and affirm'd
that he would defervedly fill it, by the
Knowledge he had gain'd in making the
Tour of *Lavinia*, and the great Infight he
had given the Learned World from the
Difcoveries he had made of the Cuftoms,
and Policies of Foreign Countries.

This *Thomafio*, had indeed great Parts to
boaft of, as well as a very Antient Defcent,
but neither his Birth nor Education, could
Attone for fome Imperfections which he too
eafily gave way to. He was Proud ; Vin-
dictive ; Impatient of Contradiction ; Deaf
to the Voice of real Danger ; and ready upon all Occafions to hearken to immaginary
Fears. He hated his Superiors, only becaufe
they were fo, and form'd Cabals againft
Men in Places of Truft, becaufe he had
not at that Time, any Dignity or Preferment offer'd Him, which He thought equal
to his Merit which he always Over-rated :
In fhort, he was always complaining of A-
bufes

bufes in the Adminiftration, that he might get into it Himfelf, and finding Fault with Officers in Power, that he might one Day be a fubject of an other Mans Envy, for the fame Preferment and Dignity.

Don Rodolpho and *Don Carlo*, were of the very fame Complexion, and by the means of a Fluency of Speech, and a diffembled Zeal for the Intereft of their Country, exclufive of their own, had fo Infinuated themfelves into the good liking of other pretended Patriots, as to have a Mighty Prevalence over them in all Matters and Caufes that were fubmitted to their Notice. They had before impos'd upon their *Electors*, by their fpecious Artifices of doing all Things for the Eafe and Advantage of their Country, of releafing them from all further Impofts and Taxes, and making Money Circulate in fuch a manner as had not been known in the Times of Tranquility and Peace: And now they were employ'd by fuch as fate at the Helm of Affairs, to gain upon the Credulous and unwary Tempers of other Members, by prevailing with them to Confent to the Donation of Immenfe Sums, fuch as before had been never granted by any preceeding Diet ; that they might thereby put a fpeedy End to the War, and give thofe that had fent them up to Town, a fpeedy poffeffion of thofe immaginary Bleffings they had fo often and fo Solemnly given them Affurances of. For

(12)

For this End, *Clubs* were form'd, Cabals inftituted, and Meetings affign'd in diverfe Places of the Metropolis, and happy was that Young Reprefentative, and at the very Summit of all Worldly fatisfaction, that could Drink Himfelf into an Efteem with *Thomafio*, could be fawn'd upon by *Rodolpho*, or Debauch'd from the Duty which he ow'd to his Country by *Carlo*. *Don Henrico* the *Scrivan* fate all this while behind the Curtain, and diffembled an Averfion to thefe Office-Haters, at the fame time, as none but he and his Accomplices were let into the Secret ; and it was no wonder that thefe, who were his Agents, carried the Point fo, as to prevail with fuch as had been drawn over into an implicite Belief of their Honour and Integrity, to make Tenders of their Lives and Fortunes to the Emprefs, and affure Her, they would fearch into the Rife of former Mifmanagements, and enable Her to wear the Imperial Diadem, with a Luftre Superior to all her Predeceffors. They promis'd likewife to put her in a way, not only to carry on the War till the Ends were obtain'd, for which it was begun, and which were no lefs than the Reftitution of feveral Kingdoms, on the Borders of the *Atlantick* Sea to their Lawful Sovereign, but the Surrender of other large Tracts of Land Scituated in that Ocean, which the Sun

takes

takes its Reft in, after the Fatigues of its Diurnal Travels, and from whence her Enemies drew thofe Immenfe Sums that enabled them to pay their Troops, and after Reiterated Defeats, to bring frefh Armies into the Field.

To give Proofs of their Loyalty and Zeal, and turn their Promifes into Performances, after the Diet had by a Publick Decreto, made a general Affeffment of Twenty Centenaries in the Hundred upon the Income of every *Villa* in the Empire; the *Mandarines* took upon them to Examine into the State of the War on the *Atlantick* Coafts. Two Legatos, or Generals, had been employ'd upon that Eftablifhment: The Firft of thefe, whofe Name was *Mordamanno*, had been recall'd Home to make way for the Laft to be put in Poffeffion of his Command, he was of an Enterprizing Genius it was true, and had done fome Things beyond their Hopes that employ'd Him: He had [thanks to his Enemies Cowardice and Confternation, more than to his own Skill in Military Affairs] with a Handful of Men made himfelf Mafter of feveral ftrong Towns, and fubdued feveral Provinces: But he was fo puff'd up and Elated with his good Fortune; as to be impatient of Advice, tho' never fo wholefome, and Averfe to all fort of Meafures that were not of his own Contrivance;

yet

yet all this while he affected to be Popular, and made it his Endeavour by a Management peculiar to Himself, rather to engage the Hearts of the *Peasants*, than In-
finuate himself into the good Graces of the
Prince, or his Nobility. Little infignifi-
cant Schemes had always more Weight
with him, than important Defigns, and
he thought it more Conducive to his own
Honour and the *Britomartian* Glory, to
raife the Siege of a poor Village that was
Beleaguer'd by the Enemies, than to give
them a Diverfion by Penetrating into the
very Heart of their Country. To give
you his Character at full length, he was
of all Perfuafions by ftarts, tho' of none
for any Continuance. His Principles alter'd with the Climate, and wherefoever
he came, he was of the Religion of the
Country. He could not be faid to be profufe of his own Money, for he fquander'd
away what belong'd to the Publick; and
to fay he was not a Man of Credit, is to
Injure him to the laft Degree, becaufe he
employ'd himfelf as much in Borrowing
Money Abroad, as he had accuftom'd himfelf to do at Home. If he was not Defeated, it was owing to his good Fortune,
rather than his Conduct, and his very Suc-
ceffes were nothing elfe, but fo many Arguments of his heedlefs Precipitancy. To
finifh his Defcription, he had it in his Power

er to reach the higheſt Pitch of Glory, but he took wrong Meaſures in the Purſuit of it, and tho' it could not be ſaid, he was ever Beaten in the Field, 'twas next to a Miracle, that he was not put to Flight, from his Sentiments in the Cabinet. Pride and Ambition that puſh'd him upon ſome Attempts, with-held him from others, and he was ſo ſtiff in his Opinion when once he had given it, that rather than not abide by it, he would run all Riſques and Hazards. This Stiffneſs and Tenaciouſneſs of Temper, made Him Sacrifice His Miſtreſſes Intereſt, and the Common Cauſe, to his own Private Reſentments, and becauſe the Lawful Sovereign of theſe Dominions would not go to his Capital by the Rout he advis'd him to take, he would no ways contribute his Aſſiſtance towards his Journey: So that when he might have put an End to the *Atlantick* War, and wholly Expell'd the Enemy from their unjuſt Uſurpations; he made it his Buſineſs to continue it, by refuſing to join thoſe Troops with his, that had advanc'd from very Remote Parts, to be ſharers in the Honour of Reducing Rebels to their due Obedience.

The Second was the Good, Old. Generous, Couragious, and Religious *Galvacio*, a Commander that always Poſtpon'd his own Intereſt to the Advantage of his Soldiers; and had nothing more at Heart,

Heart, than the Service of the Cauſe he was Glorioufly engag'd in. He had left his Native Country *Lilliania,* where he had an ample Patrimony, and a large Eſtate, on Account of Principle; and rather than not enjoy the free Exercife of that Worſhip which he was convinc'd, was the only True, he ceas'd willingly to enjoy, what God, and Nature, and the Right of a Subject entituled him to ; tho' he never abandon'd his Prince, till his Prince had bid adieu to all Law and Juſtice, and he ſaw that he muſt have abandon'd a Power that was infinitely ſuperior to all Earthly Potentates without ſuch a Removal. The Emperor *Aurantio* was poſſeſs'd of too much Merit himſelf, not to be Charm'd with the Exceſs of it in this Illuſtrious Man, and not only made him a Denizon of his Empire, and Inveſted him with a *Mandarine*'s Title but took Him as his Companion in all Military Exploits. To him it was in a great meaſure owing, that a Revolted Kingdom, which he was afterwards made Governour of, ſubmitted to his Maſters Obedience; to him and his Counſels as *Legato* from the ſame Emperor, that the *Archon* of *Sabaudia* not only kept firm to his Alliances, but acted Offenſively for the good of thoſe Princes that were Confederated with him. To him in a Word, that *Britomartia* was let into the Knowledge of
the

the *Lusitanian* Measures, and by those means not only rendred capable of opposing Force to Force, but Stratagem to Stratagem.

For some time after *Palatina* came to the Throne he led a retired Life in a little *Villa*, which was all the Estate he had purchas'd for himself during the Course of his great Employments: But as Diamonds give the greatest Lustre in Places of Obscurity, so when Removals at Court had made it necessary for true Merit to succeed, and the Patrons of Virtue had got into their Places that were the Discouragers of it, he was once more called tho' with great Reluctance by those who sate at the Helm of Government, to preside over Military Affairs, and be the Empresses Commander in Chief; in the *Lusitanian* War. His Predecessor *Scomerio*, tho' in all other Things a Consummate and experienced General, was Hot and Ambitious, and altogether disagreeable to the Natives of that Country, who would scarce allow any one to be their Equal, much less their Superior; but this good Man that was as great a Stranger to Pride, as he was to Rashness and Intemperance, no sooner came amongst them but he conciliated their Affections to Him in such a manner, that he not only retrieved their lost Honour, but gave them a Reputation they had been before unknown to. He Disciplin'd the Troops, Repell'd the E-

 nemy,

nemy, and chang'd the Countenance of the War to such a degree, that he not only preserv'd the Kingdom he came to the Rescue of, from *Hostile* Invasions ; But after various Alternatives of Conquests and Defeats, in which, he Gloriously lost an Arm, and receiv'd several other honest Wounds, he made his way maugre all opposition to the Capital of *Atalantis*, and had put the Crown of that Kingdom upon the Lawful Heirs Head ; had either *Mordamanno* done his Duty, as has been before observ'd, or *Austranio* that laid claim to it, given Ear to his repeated Solicitations of *Coming*, *Seeing*, and *Conquering*. Hence it was that the Throne of *Atalantis* was further to be disputed and contended for, by the Two Royal Rivals that were in Arms to determine the Succession, and *Galvacio*, after many fruitless Attempts to recover that lost Opportunity, thro' the negligence of those Councillors who attended upon the Young Prince, and the want of Succours from *Britomartia*, was forc'd to be upon the Defensive, after he had again signaliz'd his Courage by the loss of an Eye, in a very fatal Encounter, which had ended in a Glorious Victory on his side, had not *Austranio* drawn off the Flower of his Forces from the Army, Two Days before the Battle, and abandon'd them to an Enemy that was much superior in Number.

Yet

Yet notwithstanding all these Hardships
and Difficulties, he struggled with them so
as to continue Transacting Affairs with the
utmost Prudence and Dispatch, and tho,
Vanquish'd, made it appear by his Assidu-
ity and Address, by his Care and Prudence,
that the Conqueror's might in their Turns
lose the Day upon a less Fortunate Occasion : But neither his great Age, the Wounds
he had receiv'd, nor his Integrity of Soul
were of any use to Him at this juncture;
and it was in vain to plead that his Hoary
Locks, his Honourable Scars, and his un-
suspected Fidelity, might excuse him from
any Publick Censure ; The *Mandarines* were
prepossess'd in favour of the profligate, *Li-
bidinous* and Itinerant, *Mordamanno*; and the
Wrong'd *Galvacio,* had the Misfortune to
see himself Accus'd and Traduc'd to the
Empress His Mistress, for feign'd Crimes
and Misdemeanors, while his Antagonist
had the Thanks of the Nobles for those
that were real.

As the *Mandarines* had begun their Ses-
sion with this remarkable Instance, of Prejudice and Injustice; so the *Proatins* resolv'd not to be behind Hand with them,
in Actions of the same Complexion, though
relating to Affairs of a contrary Nature.
They had promis'd the Empress to trace
the source of that great Evil, the National
Debts, and not being able to be as good as

their

their Words, fell foul upon the Management of the *Thalaſſiano*, and after voting
that there had been notorious Imbezelments
of the Proviſions and Scandalous Abuſes in
that Branch of the Adminiſtration, caus'd
one of their own Members to be declar'd
incapable of Sitting amongſt them, for his
being concerned in thoſe pretended Miſ-
management, and order'd Him with ſeveral others, whoſe only Fault was for contracting with the Government on the ſame
Foot as their Predeceſſors, and as it were
ſupporting it, by entruſting it with their
Stocks, and giving Credit for what, upon
other Occaſions, it was won't to pay down
ready Money. Tho' theſe Proſecutions
came to nothing, and the Perſons order'd
to be ſo ſerv'd, continued their dealing on
upon the old Bottom, yet, as it was intended, they made a great noiſe in the Cities,
Towns and Provinces of the Empire, from
whence theſe Deputies were ſent up to the
Diet, and they gain'd thereby ſuch Ap-
plauſes and good Likeing, as rendred all
their Proceedings acceptable to the Populace, who look no farther than the Super-
ficies of Things, and are more taken with
Shadows and Appearances, than Realties
and ſubſtantial Truths. This was a great
Inducement for theſe Inveſtigators of Frauds
and Abuſes, to cortinue their Enquiries into other Branches of Miſmanagements and

Miſ-

Mifapplications ; and after they had taken
Care to make a *Decreto* in Favour of themfelves, that their Clubs might be fupplied
with good Wines, by taking off the Prohi-
bition,that fuffer'd them not to be Imported
from an Enemies Country; and had ferioufly
fet their Heads a Work, to endear themfelves with the *Sacrifto's* of the *Montalti*
Party, by promulging a Law to Build them
more Places of Worfhip, to fpread their
Arbitrary Tenents in, they drew up a long
Remonftrance to Her Imperial Majefty, of
vaft Sums not Accounted for, by the late
Officers of Her *Fifcalio*, illegal Practices by
Mifapplications of the Publick Money,
Scandalous Embezelments, Immenfe Debts
arifing from thence, and the entertaining
of poor Starv'd Creatures, who Fled to them
for Refuge, from an Infulting and Invading
Enemy, even when thefe Objects of
Compaffion were their Allies and Confederates, and the Opulence and ftrength of a
Nation depends upon the Number and Increafe of its Inhabitants. Unwarrantable
Proceedings of Arbitrary Denizations, relating to Cities and Bodies Corporate, for which
the Outed Miniftry were loaded with Repro-
ches, and rendred Odious to the whole Empire *came alfo in play* ; when to the very Day
which this Hiftory was Written in, (and
this was Written after they had clofed their
Seffion) they have neither been Summon'd

before

before the Tribunal to anfwer for the Crimes
they have been fo peremptorily Charged
with, nor permitted to give Proofs of their
Innocence, and difengage themfelves in the
Prefence of the fupreme Authority, from
all thofe Scandalous and falfe Imputations,
which, by the means of their not being
called to account, they continued being
fubjected to.

Obloquies, and fubtile Invectives and Infinuations were the Weapons that were
made ufe of to deftroy the Reputation of
fuch, as would not come into the fame
Meafures with thefe *Proatins*, fince they
could not but know, that a fair and equitable Tryal, would *acquit* thofe who might
continue *fufpected* without one. They were
likewife fenfible that the Caufe, by being
brought into a Court of Judicature, would
not only undoubtedly be loft, but endanger
the lofs of fuch profitable Places, as the chief
Leaders of them were poffefs'd of, and their
Credit with the People, whofe Eye-fight
might be cleared up, and rendred capable
of forming a right Judgment between the
Accufers Articles, and the Sincerity of the
Patriots that were *Accufed*. Wherefore,
tho' they came to ftinging Refolutions a-
bout Publick Abufes, thofe whom they Voted Guilty, were not only not Perfecuted,
but employ'd to Contract on with the Government upon the fame Bottom as formerly;
and tho' it was given out among the Populace,

(23)

lace, that fuch and fuch *Madarines* would
be called to Account, for prodigious Mifapplications and Amaffments of national
Treafure for their own private Ufes, 'twas
thought more advifeable by thofe in Power
to content themfelves with Stymatizing
them, with the Infamous Character of being *Enemies to their Country*; which was
much eafier than giving themfelves the
Trouble of proving them fo. By thefe
means the Keeper of the *Tulliano*, or the
State Prifon, (of the fame Nature with our
Tower of *London*) who had form'd to himfelf
very Profitable Conceptions, and was big
with Hopes of Enriching himfelf, with the
Spoils of his new Imaginary Tenants, was
wholly difappointed ; and the Common People had the Mortification to fee their Expectations of feveral Important Executions,
likewife Fruftrated and Defeated.

But tho' no Criminal Procefs was yet
form'd againft Men of Worth and Integrity, and the *Proatins* had it not amongft o-
ther Privileges of the General *Diet* to be
Judges, as well as *Accufers* of fuch as were
not Members of that Illuftrious Affembly,
or laid no Claim to an Admittance amongft
them ; yet their Authority was Uncontroulable in relation to Punifhments among
themfelves, and Decifions in Contraverted
Elections. In thefe, it appear'd how the
Old *Britomartian* Spirit was decay'd and
loft

loft, and how that Unbyafs'd Honefty and Honour, which us'd to bear Rule, and prefide in all their Determinations was funk into the meaneft and moft fordid Compliances. It was not enough that this or that Deputy was Recomended to his Seat in the *Diet*, by all the Virtues which Humanity could be invefted with, that he was Wealthy, Juft and Generous; that he had the Higheft Regard for the Emprefs, was truly affectionate to the Welfare, and obfervant of the Conftitutions of the Empire; that he was fam'd for Capacity and Prudence, and adorn'd with all Moral and Political Acquirements, unlefs he came thither to make his Court to the New-Favourites, and to Complement them with the Surrender of his Principles upon all Occafions. To Petition againft one that would not give into the New Schemes, was inftantly to be admitted into his Place, and there fcarce needed any other Evidence to prove a Man duely made choice of, than that he was not fo. In fome Cafes, *Forty* was lefs than *Fifteen*, and *Five* more in Number, than *Twenty*; fo that the Ordinary Rules of *Arithmetick*, were quite out of Date with them, and it was not he that was fent up to ferve his Country by the moft Votes was allow'd to be regularly Chofen, but he that had the moft Votes when he came there. Infomuch, that it was wifely obferved by a

Rejected

Rejected Member; That it fignified little or nothing to be made Choice of, in fuch Places as the Laws Directed, fince the Right of Electing feem'd wholly to be Transferr'd elfewhere, and without makeing Intereft in the *Pretorian* Hall, all the Intereft that could be made in the Country, would be of no ufe to any one.

Such Proceedings as thefe could not fail of putting them into a Capacity of ridding their Hands of all manner of Oppofition, fo that the *Montalti*, for that was the prevailing Party, could not but obtain what ever they puſh'd at, by a vaft Majority. Therefore, after they had Voted the Empire to be much more in Debt, than it really was by many Millions, tho' it could not be otherwife than in Debt, by Reafon of the Deficiences of the Funds, and feveral contigent Expences that were charged upon every Branch of the Revenue, and might happen under the moft Prudent and Careful Adminiftration; they very wifely Reflected within themfelves, that the only way to make their black Affertions ftick upon the *Old* Managers, was to do fomething to advance the Reputation of the *New*. Several Projections were confulted for this End; at laft an *Old-Caft* Expedient was laid hold, after all other Ways and Means were releas'd from their Deliberation; and it was refolv'd that thofe Debts fhould be *Paid*, and that

that without Burthening the Empire with fresh Imposts and Taxes, and even without *Money*. What remain'd for the *Proatins* to do, was to make good their Resolutions by passing a *Decreto* for that Purpose, the Advantages of which were so surprizing, that few or none understood them, tho' Multitudes blindly closed in with the Proposals, and gave up the Principal of what was Legally due to them, for the bare Expectation of being one Day or other Paid the Interest. This, in the Language of those Days was called *paying of Debts*, when in our Dialect, it would have been *running farther in*, and the *Proatins* had the Art and engaging Persuasions, to make the Poor Gull'd Creditors believe, that *Building Castles in the Air*, was making Good and *Legal Settlements*, and *Hunting* after *Impossibilities*, was to obtain the Fruition of inestimable Advantages.

The Trading Part of the Empire, had been highly disoblig'd by the late Promotions at Court, while the Landed Interest grew daily more and more Prevalent, and since it was owing to the *Loans* of the First, that many considerable Victories and Important Conquests had been obtain'd over the Enemy; it was but Justice to make a shew of bringing them in, as it were sharers with the Last, for their Readiness to Assist and Extricate them out of all Difficulties upon

emergent

emergent Occafions. There was a certain Tract of Land, faid to lie *Southward* of the accidental Ocean, whofe Rich Veins were reported to Teem and be Impregnated with nothing but gold and Silver. Hither it was that *the Attention of their Creditors was to be drawn.* They were to be told Wonders of the Soil, and the Wealth and the Humanity of the Inhabitants ; the Simplicity of their Conduct ; and their open and frank way of giving Entertainment to Strangers. How that before all Nations in the Univerfe, they were Ambitious of Cultivating a ftrict Friendfhip with the *Britomartian* State, and how it was nothing more, than to Embark in an Adventure of *Commerce,* and to be put into the certain Poffeffion of a large Extent of Dominion which was no ways to be doubted ; and it was but to touch upon thefe Coafts, and to return frighted with Gems and Pretious Stones, and laden with what would bring Millions into the Adventurers Exchequer.

The Hook that was cover'd with fo tempting and inviting a Bait, drew abundance of greedy Mercinaries into the Snare that was laid for them, and thofe that prepar'd it, had the Satisfaction of feeing whole fhoals of the Unthinking Fry, made a Sacrifice to their Vanity and Ambition, and precipitated head-long upon impracticable Defigns, that could not but end in
their

their Ruin and Confusion. Instead of Purchasing the Wealth they were allured with, the poor deluded Wretches had nothing but Poverty to contend with, and in Lieu of a Hospitable Reception from their pretended Friends, they were to find nothing but Hostilities from open and declared Enemies ; yet notwithstanding all these unsurmountable Difficulties; those that were at the Head of the Project were cry'd up, and applauded for the vast Utility and Benefit that would arise from it, and Hirelings were employ'd to distribute and spread about their Praises, that what should have rendred them hateful to all Mankind, made them the Objects of their Esteem, ard even the very Ruin of their Country Men and Fellow Subjects, tended to the Inhancement and Increase of their Honour and Reputation.

To ingratiate themselves yet more with People that hug'd their own Destruction, and as it were *Enjoy'd* their very Ruin ; as they had impos'd upon such as dealt in *Traffick*, so they would do by those that Administer'd in *Holy* Matters : And it was one and the same thing while their Hands were in, and they were wholly taken up in Acts of Beneficence, to involve themselves over Head and Ears as to go any length cut of their Depth. They were conscious to themselves, that by the means of the *Sacristo's*, who

who had made Intereſt for them with the
Bigots that were under their Care and Di-
rection ; they had been rais'd to the Stati-
ons they were then in, and could not but
know, that without ſome Advances in their
Behalf, they might alter their Notes, and
diſpoſe themſelves in Favour of other Candidates at a New Election. They therefore
before the riſing of the Diet, made a *Decreto* for Building ſeveral new Edifices, for the
Exerciſe of theNationalReligion,which was
now ſaid to be in the *Zenith* of its Glory,
and its moſt Flouriſhing State, and this ſo
far added to their Strength and Intereſt ;
that whereas, by their former Generoſity
they had Conciliated the good Will and
Affections of the looſer, and more Robuſt
Part of Mankind, the Rabble, who vouch-
ſafed to Honour 'em with their Approbation ; ſo now by this laſt Proof of their Un-
wearied Proſecution of Works of Manifi-
cence, they had the Hearts of all the Old
Men and Women at their Diſpoſal, and
got into the good liking of many a Young
Damſel, who was oblig'd to Diſſemble a
great Value for *Spiritual* Gifts, while She
had at Heart Donations and Benevolences
that were altogether *Carnal.*

Theſe, and the like ſpecious Appearan-
ces of Affection to their Country, and Good
Will to thoſe that Entruſted them with the
Conſervation of their Liberties ; (for in

Reality

Reality they had little or no Regard for either) employ'd the Diet for more than Half a Year; when the Emprefs *Palatina* difmifs'd them to their refpective Places of Abode, till the Seafon for making the Campaign was over, and She fhould ftand in need of frefh Supplies to carry on the War, which had thitherto been Conducted with great Honour and Advantage to the *Britomartian* State, and its Allies and Confederates. In the mean time the Outed Courtiers continued to have the Mortification of feeing their Intereft grow Weaker and Weaker; while thofe that were Invefted with their Offices, gain'd frefh Accefs of Strength, by giving Places of Truft, to fuch Members of the General Diet, who before their being chofen had made Proteftations of their being Candidates for that Dignity, folely for the *Good of their Country*, not for any *Views* or *Hopes* of *private Advantage*. Thefe Men, as has been before Obferved. Compofed a fort of a Club, the very Effence of whofe Inftitution, was an Abhorrence of all State-Preferments, and the Profeffion of Self-Denial in the moft Abftracten Senfe; But thofe who Sate at the Helm of Affairs, having got into the right Knowledge of their Pulfes, foon had a Remedy at Hand to Cure them of this Diftemper, and by gaining over Two or Three of their Principal Leaders by very engaging Rewards

wards, had it in their Power to find, that the Confciences of moft of the Reft were as Malleable as theirs, who had before made a Tender of their Principles to the Service of the State.

Among thefe, the loud and Talkative *Ignifacio* was a Perfon whom *Palatina*'s Minifters had in their Eye. He was Rich and Fearlefs, of great Refolution, in Detecting Mifmanagements of State, and by the forward Zeal he had fhewn, in making others guilty of Frauds and Abufes ; was thought fitting to be made a Profelyte by fome profitable Employment, that by Contracting that Guilt himfelf, he might flacken his Enquiries of that Nature, and be more remifs in future Inveftigations. But as this was never to be brought about by any Office that had not a very Confiderable Salary annex'd to it, (for he was of too Covetous a Nature to be fatisfied with fmall *Perquifites* Himfelf, tho' he held the Receipt of any to be unlawful in Others) fo it was a Work of fometime, before he could be Invefted with any Thing that bore Proportion to his Vanity and Ambition : What he fpoke in the Diet, was always deliver'd by him with great Emotion and Vehemence; this Gain'd Him no fmall Credit and Intereft among fome Men, who always give into the Belief of the Juftice of a Caufe, from the Vigour that was

fhewn

fhewn in adhering to it, and made Him popular amongft the Younger Members, who
Meafur'd his Capacity by his Rafhnefs, that
was miftaken for Courage, and fet a Value
upon every thing, rather for its Acrimony
and Malice, than its Solidity and Senfe.
Wherefore he was to be Carefs'd and fent
Home to the Province, he Reprefented with
Affurances that Care fhould be taken of
providing for fuch Extraordinary Merit, as
foon as Occafion fhould Offer : Becaufe,
tho' the Gentlemen at the Head of the New
Scheme were fully bent upon making a
through Change in all the Offices of Truft,
yet it was Prudence in them to do it in fuch
a manner, that fhould make them leaft fufpected of Injuftice, and capable of fhewing fome Grounds for every Removal; and
thofe whofe Prefervation and Eftablifhment, wholly lies in Alterations of this Nature, feldom want Pretences (which they
call Reafons) for making them.

   Don Ricardino likewife a Mandarine of
the Firft Rank, from being a great ftickler
againft the Principles in Vogue, and a declared Enemy to any thing that bore the
Refemblance of Unlimited Power, was prevail'd with to bid adieu to his Old Friends,
and enter into Engagements with thofe
he formerly had the greateft Averfion to.
Not that the Party whofe Profelyte he was,
could promife to themfelves any great Ac-
ceffion

ceſſion of Credit from his Defection, but it gain'd ſtrength by it, which was to be purchas'd at any Rate, ſince, by how much the nearer to an Equality in Number, the Nobles, who were faſly called the *Faction*, came up with their Antagoniſts, by ſo much the more did it behove the *Montalti* to weaken and impair their Intereſt, by drawing them over to the Oppoſite ſide.

Power, Profit and all other tempting Advantages were on their ſide, whoſe Banner he was Liſted then under; and *Don Ricardino* who Inherited his Fathers Qualities with his Eſtate and Title broke thro' all Obligations that were never ſo binding, to encreaſe that Wealth which was great enough to ſatisfie any ones Deſires, who was without Iſſue-Male asHe was.He forgot how the Emperor *Aurantio*, whom he then Deſerted (tho' Dead) in his beſt Friends, had heap'd unmerited Favours upon Him; how he had taken Him as it were into his Boſom, from the Company of Gameſters and Leud Aſſociates; how he had reconcil'd Him into an Allowance from his Fathers Patrimony; how he had made Him a *Prefecto* of his own Body Guards : In a word, he ceas'd to remember every thing that was paſt, that he might have Room to charge his Memory with what was to come, and allur'd with the delightful Proſpect of *Tinſel'd* Grandeur, left adhering to the Cauſe of

C   plain,

plain, open and difinterefted Integrity.
The Places of Prince *Mirabel*, like the Branches of a fpacious Oak that had long been
the Pride and Glory of the whole Foreft,
were now for his paft Services to be Lopp'd
off, and parcel'd out amongft thofe that en-
vied Him the Rewards of his Juft Merits,
and that of *Archi-Tormentario* carried fuch
Charms with it, that he would have com-
plyed with any thing, nay, jump'd over
a Stick, for the Attainment of it. At the
very Moment of his Ungrateful Revolt,
he was made a Tribuno of the beft Corps
of Cavalry that was in the Empire, and to
Eftablifh him in it; he had likewife this
additional Poft, which was the Chief Dignity that could be acquir'd, confer'd upon
Him: So that the Renown'd and Victorious *Mirabel*, that had Triumph'd over all
Hoftilities Abroad; faw Himfelf *Trick'd*
and Infulted by his Enemies at Home, and
he that was moft unjuftly traduced and vilified for a *Plunderer* and a *Robber* of the
Publick, was himfelf ftrip'd and deprived
of thofe Honours which were juftly his
own, from the moft approv'd Fidelity, and
Confummate Experience,to gratifie the Ambition of privatePerfons.OLoyaltywhere was
thy Reward, O Valour where was thy Recompence! Did *Mirabel* for this, wear out an
advanc'd age inCamps,and for 10Years together,run thehazard of converfing abroadwith
Blood

Blood and Slaughter ?   Did *Ricardino* for
this, fpend more than double the Number
in Luxury and Eafe, and Fatigue Himfelf
in making no other Conquefts than in Engagements with the Ladies ?   Such are the
Retributions of fome People, to the moft
Eminent and Unexampled Defert, and fuch
their profufe and lavifh Benefactions, to
the moft inconfiderable, and moft undeferv-
ing of their Favours.

To return to the Proceedings of the *Diet*,
which at the accuftomed Seafon of the
Year fate again :   They were told from the
Throne, that during their Recefs Propofals had been made by the Enemy, of Entring into a Treaty upon fuch a Footing, as
gave great Grounds to hope, would end in
an Honourable and Lafting Peace, and that
the only way to make that Peace advantagious, was to raife proper Funds for making
another Campaign ; that if the Negotiations which were upon the Point of Com-
mencing, whofe particulars would in due
time be laid before them, fhould not have
their defired Effect, it might appear
they were prepared on their fide to force
the *Lillianians* to accept of Terms that
were Juft and reafonable.   This, with
many Indulgent Affurances of Favour and
Affection to Her loving Subjects, and Regard for the Interefts of the Potentates in
Alliance with Her, was the Subftance of

C 2   the

the Empreſſes Speech from the Throne, and both Orders of that Auguſt Aſſembly, to ſhew themſelves ready to make all poſſible Returns, anſwer'd thoſe Aſſurances with Promiſes of inviolable Obedience, and the utmoſt Aſſiſtance they could give Her upon ſo emergent an Occaſion. Tho' it was to be Obſerved, that there was ſome Difference between them in the Terms of their Reſpective Harrangues, for the *Mandarines*, who were truly ſenſible of the Reaſons that were given for their Entring into the War, beſought Her Imperial Majeſty not to put an End to it, till the Kingdom of *Atalantis* with all the Dominions belonging to it, was reſtored to its Lawful Owner ; while the *Proatins*, who were without any Reſerve in the Court Intereſt, entirely left it to the Will and Pleaſure of the Crown to Exerciſe its Prerogative of making Peace in what Terms and Conditions the Prince that wore it ſhould think fit. Not that it was carried amongſt one or the other without a Debate upon the Queſtion, to Act this or that way ; ſince the firſt Reſolution was very ſtrenuouſly oppos'd by ſeveral Noble Perſons, in particular by the Chief Miniſter and his Dependents, and the laſt was ſpoken againſt with great Vehemence and Indignation, (tho' not by the like Number of Gentlemen) by ſuch as had the good of the Empire more at Heart,

than

than the Eſtabliſhment and Impunity of
the Miniſtry then in Being.

Some Private Articles of a Negotiation,
that was intended to have been kept ſecret, till Men's Minds were form'd and diſ-
poſed to receive them, had crept Abroad,
and it was in every ones Mouth, upon what
Conditions they were to come to an Accommodation with the Common Enemy.
In this Man's Face was to be ſeen a Pre-
ſumptuous and Haughty Joy for the near
Approach of ſo ineſtimable a Bleſſing ; in
that Man's, the deepeſt Concern and Sor-
row for ſo unpremeditated and haſty a Procedure. One took it upon Truſt, that the
Peace would of neceſſity be *Safe* and *Honourable*, becauſe ſuch and ſuch Perſons
were employ'd in Treating of it ; another
was of a contrary Opinion, and juſtly concluded it could not deſerve that Appellati-
on, becauſe it infinitely fell ſhort of what
he had promiſed himſelf by the Continuance of the War. Of this Opinion among
the *Proatins*, were all thoſe who were
diſatisfied with the late Alterations, and
had a true Senſe of the Regard which
ſhould be ſhewn to Treaties and Alliances.
The Polite, Gallant, and immoveable *Suavilinguo*, ſpoke all that the moſt Conſum-
mate Experience approv'd Eloquence, and
Irriſiſtable Truth could furniſh an Argument with, for carrying on the War, and

laid

laid before them in the moſt Pathetick manner, the Miſchiefs that would unavoidably
follow ſo degenerate and ſordid a Con-
" deſcention. Far be it, *ſaid he*, far from
" Conquerors, Oh! far from *Brito-*
" *martians*, to think of giving up the Price
" of ſo many Victories to a Perfidious and
" Cruel Enemy. Shall *Atalantis* be aban-
" don'd to the Poſſeſſion of an Uſurper,
" or Kingdoms that have coſt us ſo much
" Blood and Treaſure, and are juſt falling
" into our Hands be relinquiſh'd at the
" Will of a petulant and Capricious Mi-
" niſtry? Our Liberties, our Lives, our
" Eſtates, our Altars are endanger'd by
" theſe Proceedings, and We cannot anſ-
" wer to Poſterity the Wrongs We are
" now doing them. Has the Great *Mira-*
" *bel* for this Headed your Armies, and
" thro' Thouſands of the Slain, led them
" annually on to repeated Conqueſts and
" Triumphs? Has he toil'd to compleat
" your Eaſe and Quiet, and inur'd Himſelf
" to Hazards and Fatigues for your Con-
" tentment? Has he reduced Cities by
" his Valour and Counſels, to be the Pur-
" chaſe of thoſe he took them from, and
" made Towns open their Gates to Him,
" to give them up again into their Hands
" that have no Right to them? Could a
" Conquer'd People do more than ſubmit
" themſelves to the Mercy of the Con-
quereors,

" querors, and shall we that have the De-
" nomination of the Last, ignomiously sub-
" mit to be in the Condition of the First ?
" No, let us keep in Remembrance the
" Glory and Success of our Nation and our
" Arms, and ever set before us the Advan-
" tages we are now Masters of : Let us
" look up to those Names we have Sworn
" by, and Invoke their Celestial Aid and
" Assistance who are Witnesses to an Alli-
" ance, we cannot without Infraction of
" Oaths any ways recede from; let us rather
" think of Ways and Means to compel
" the Enemy, to be thankful for what
" Terms we shall vouchsafe to give 'em,
" than make our selves the Reproach and
" Talk of the whole Universe by receiving
" Conditions from them.

Hamenio, whose Hereditary Zeal for the
Cause of Liberty made him walk a-breast
with his renown'd Ancestors, spoke to the
same purpose: as did also the florid and
sage *Lecamero*; but Force of Expression
ceas'd to have its due Weight; and it was
not in the Power of the most excelling
Orator to perfuade a Majority to give Ear
to the Voice of Truth and Reason. De-
monstration that was ever the most infal-
lible Criterion, was no longer of any Authority, and Golden Mifts had so dazzled
their Eyes, that they could not see into
the greatest Certainties. In a word, there

was

was a Neceffity of a Peace to fecure the
Projectors of the New Scheme; and thofe
that gave their Votes for it out of Neceffity, very much out number'd thofe generous Patriots, who would not fuffer the
Publick Good to give way to their Private
Occafions. Thefe were call'd *Enemies to
the Temple*, and Haters of the Worfhip
that was celebrated in it; but thefe, when
a fit Opportunity prefented it felf, and
there was no Danger of exafperating fuch
as could not comply with it, fhew'd
themfelves greater Friends to the Religion
in Vogue, than the Pretenders to the ftric-
teft Exercife of it: and gave Being to a
Decreto that fecur'd it beyond any Poffibility of being endanger'd.

Lateolo was the Perfon that firft mov'd
for this Edict; a Man ever till upon this Occafion reckon'd entirely devoted to the
Montaltis's Opinion, and always Bigotted
rather than adhering to their Intereft. But
in procefs of Time through the means of
cooler Thoughts, and a due confideration
of Things and Purpofes, he came into
more moderate and advifeable Meafures.
Not that he altogether chang'd his Principles, or departed from his former Affertions, as his late Friends and Affociates gave
out, (for he had from the Beginning vigo-
roufly efpous'd the *Atalantick* War, and
Voted for its continuance till the Kingdom
of

of that Name, with all its Dependencies
fhould bewrefted from theHandsof him that
Ufurp'd it) but grown wifer by Conviction, and a certain view of fome unjuftifiable
Defigns that were carried on under, the
Cloak of Religion and Loyalty, he dif-
claim'd the Practitioners of fuch Wicked
Arts, and maugre all their Temptations
to abide by them, reconciled Himfelf to
that Integrity and Juftice, without which,
no Man can be truly Great, howfoever,
laden and adorn'd with Honours and Titles.

Hereupon, thofe who could not confute
his Reafons for relinquifhing their fide,
fet their Hirelings at Work to ridicule and
make little of his Perfon, and becaufe Nature, that had been indulgent to Him in the
laft Degree, in the Brightnefs of his Soul,
had not been fo Profufe to Him in the Ele-
gancies of his Body ; but had given Him a
Swarthy Countenance, they quarrel'd with
his Complexion, and difpers'd Libels relating to his Singularity of Drefs : A Method one would think more proper to be
taken, in order to render Him Contempti-
ble and Odious to the Ladies than the
Men, who form their Approbation or
Diflike, not from the Beauties or Deformi-
ties of the Body, but from the Graces and
Imperfections of the Mind.

So confiderable a Profelyte to a Caufe
that had fo much Juftice of its fide, could
not

not but add Weight to it by other Converts,
and several *Mandarines* with whom his Example was of great Authority fol ow'd his
Steps ; In so much, that those of the contrary Party judg'd themselves in Danger
of being out-number'd, and had violent
Suspicions, which were no ways ill grounded, that the Face of Affairs might be liable
to Alterations in favour of their Enemies.
Extraordinary Cases, said they, require extraordinary Remedies, and immediately
the Friends to the new Settlement were
Conven'd to Debate about necessary Expedients to defeat the Designs of such Members as were for reinstating Things upon
the Old Establishment. *Novicius,* and his
Creatures knew full well, that immediate
Imprisonment was design'd for Him, if
those who could not give into his Projects
should obtain a Majority, and therefore
since there was but a little distance between
the Prisons and the Graves of great and
Ambitious Men, and he had no ways Merited the Compassion of the Outed Courtiers, he prevail'd with the Empress *Palatina*
by new Promotions to strengthen his Interest, which was effectually done by many
Voices in the *Diet* that were wholly at his
Disposal. Those who pretended to defend
this Notable Resolution, said that it was
the undoubted Prerogative of the Imperial
Dignity, to make as many *Mandarines* as
those

thofe that were Invefted with it pleafed,
and that the Reafon of placing that Power
in the Crown, was that the Emperours of
Britomartia might have it in their Power
to Reward Secret, as well as Publick Services ; that therefore thofe who were diffa-
tisfied, ought not in the leaft to repine, had
the Emprefs made twice the Number She
did. On the other fide it was urg'd, that
Her Imperial Majefty had an undoubted
Right of Creating as many *Mandarines* as
She pleas'd ; yet thofe in Authority under
Her, might be called to a very ftrict and
heavy Account for advifing Her to Abufe
that Right : That Peace and War were
the Prerogatives of the Throne, and yet
the engaging in a Ruinous War, or
making a Treacherous Peace, were Things
that no Miniftry efcaped harmlefs. To
this it was added, that pouring a Number
into the Diet to ferve a Turn, was making
that Diet a Property to the Court, and
that tho' thefe might have been advanced
to reward paft Services, this might be a
Precedent for Bribing others to future ones,
which would be of dangerous Confequences. For if in the Reign of fuch a Prince,
this Procedure was exclaim'd againft, becaufe it was new, what would the Cry
have been had it been done in a Sufpicious
Reign ? Thus it was held for a bold Action, tho' no one difputed the Prudence of

it, becaufe it was made ufe of in fo difficult a Conjuncture.

The Point being Weather'd, which feem'd
to threaten the Favourite Court er's Exalted Grandeur with immediate Diffolution,
and future Storms amply provided againft
by the new Creations, it was eafie to fee
they would not be wanting to themfelves
in making a right Ufe of that Influence
they had over the Diet in general : For
as *Novicius* had fecur'd himfelf from all Attempts amongft thofe of his own Clafs, fo
Care was taken among the *Proatins*, who
needed no extraordinary Meafures to be
brought into an entire Refignation to his
Will and Pleafure, to pufh them upon frefh
Enquiries relating to Abufes and Corrupti-
ons. It was not enough that the Valiant
and Irreproachable Prince *Mirabel* was di-
vefted of his Employments, and difpoffefs'd
of the Commands which he did Honour to,
by his Acceptance, but he muft alfo be render'd Criminal to take off the Odium of
their Ingratitude for his paft Services ;
Therefore, when they could faften no ill
Practices upon Him of a higher Nature,
tho' they gave out, that his Intentions were
to be a General for Life, and like the Renown'd *Cæfar's*, afpiring to the perpetual
Dictatorfhip, they forgot themfelves fo far,
as to defcend into Accufations of *Petty Lar-
cenie*, and to charge Him with converting

Triffles

Triffles to his own Ufe, that were never defign'd for any others, but had always been allow'd to his Predeceffors as Perquifites of his Office.

Nor could all the Mufick that dwelt upon *Suavilinguo*'s Harmonious Tongue preferve that Honeft, that Uncorrupted Patriot, from the Wrongs of Violence and Injuftice. The Truths he fpoke were too Pungent to be born with, and a Superiority of Numbers was not efteem'd a fufficient Security for thofe of the contrary Party, while this Man, this one Man, continued to have a Voice in the Diet. The lofs of his Places had no ways impair'd his Courage and Refolution, it had rather added frefh Vigour to it, and he was fo far from being deprefs'd or caft down by his own Injurious Treatment, that it warm'd him into the higheft Refentments, for that of his Country, and always made him foremoft in oppofing whatfoever bore any Tendency to its Det.ement. Yet was this Lover of the Land of his Nativity, this Affertor of its Rights and Immunities, this Defender of its Antient Conftitution, Traduc'd, Vilified, and Adjudg'd without Caufe. He that was abhorrent of an Ungenerous Act, was called in Queftion for Bribery, and who never was, one Centenarie, the Richer, for Fingering the Publick Money, declared Guilty of Defrauding the Publick, and of

Forfeiting

Forfeiting his Place in the Diet. As a further inftance of his Enemies Inveteracy, he was likewife committed Prifoner to the *Tullianio,* as if one Punifhment was not fufficient for one Offence, had it been real and not imaginary; and he that ftood up for the Liberties of the whole World, ought to be Imprifon'd for his Noble and Freeborn Sentiments.

But it was not enough to make ufe of the greateft Severities to their own Country-Men, the *Proatins* would likewife give Inftances of their Barbarity to diftrefs'd Foreigners. The Defolations of War and the moft extream Poverty, were no Inducements to Charity, and thofe poor Wretches that by a former Edict had leave to fettle in *Britomartia* for Reafons of State, which always allow'd the Power and Wealth of a Nation to confift in the Number of its Inhabitants, were now for the quite contrary Reafons to be no longer Tolerated amongft them, tho' the Subjects of a Prince in Alliance with the Emprefs *Palatina,* and Men whofe Labour and Induftrious Wants might have Cultivated the Ground, and improv'd Tracts of Land, that without them would continue to lie fallow.

It was alfo thought fitting to find occafions of Quarelling with another Potentate their faft Confederate, that they might have the better Grounds to carry on a Trea-

ty

ty without Him ; they therefore Voted the *Mandarine Hortentio,* and all others concern'd with Him, Enemies to their Country, for having Be-friended it, in making a League for its greater Security in the Preſervation of its Neighbouring States, ſet themſelves Heartily at Work to give Reaſons for ſo doing ; which however difficult to be pro- duc'd, appear'd afterwards in a long Com- plaint, That the *Britomartians* had furniſh'd Two Thirds more, that it was Stipulated with their Allies to ſend into the Field, and had out gone their juſt Proportions of the War ſeveral Millions of Centenaries. Theſe Aſſertions were made Publick with a long Catalogue of Particulars, to incenſe the whole Empire againſt the Perſons complain'd of, tho' it miſs'd of its intended Effect, and made appear from Anſwers, that were made to it, and expoſtulatory Letters upon that Head, that they had not only come up to the Tenour of each reſpective Agree- ment, but had in many Inſtances exerted themſelves beyond their Abilities for the good of the Common Cauſe. As theſe Re- monſtances againſt their Proceedings, ſet their Deſigns in a full Light, ſo the *Proa- tins* were not backward to ſhew their Re- ſentments ; and accordingly Repreſented their Senſe of theſe pretended Impoſitions, in ſo lively and Pathetick a manner, that it gave new Life to their drooping Cauſe, and

and reviv'd that Popular Indignation that had before departed from the Spirits of the Multitude. Infomuch, that thofe who juft before were look'd upon, and Efteem'd Friends for contributing their utmoft, to-wards carrying on the War, in Conjunction with them, were now reckon'd their worft Enemies, for Obftructing a Peace, that would put an End to the Ruins and Depredations that were faid to be made by their Accomplices, upon the Publick Treafure.

In the mean time, the Negotiations of Peace that were then upon the Anvil, feem'd to take but a very flow Turn from the Meafures of the *Lillianian* Deputies, who inftead of Anfwering the Demands of the Perfons employ'd to Treat with them, went on in their Old Road of Prevarication, and gave in fuch Propofals, as look'd rather to come from a Conqueror that prefcrib'd Conditions, than a Prince who had fo earneftly and fo meanly Supplicated for Terms of Agreement in all the Courts of his Enemies. The *Mandarines*, like great and good Men, who had at Heart the Profperity of their Native Country, and the fafety of their Allies, receiv'd thefe Offers as it juftly became them, and declared that thofe Propofitions ought to be rejected with the Higheft Indignation, and that it plainly appear'd, *Lilliania*, had no other Defigns in view than to divide the Allies,&c. To this End, they Petition'd

tition'd Her Imperial Majefty, to reject them
as Derogatory to Her Honour, and the
Glory of Her Arms, with Promifes of ftanding by Her, with their Lives and Fortunes,
till fuch a Peace fhould be obtain'd, that
was Safe and Honourable for the Empire,
and all its Allies. The *Proatins* indeed
made no Remonftrance againft them, nor
applyed to the Throne on this Account, but
as they had before left the whole to *Pali-
tina*'s Choice, fo they now Acquiefc'd in
her Thoughts concerning it, very cunning-
ly fuggefting that as in moft Barguins thofe
who Sell, and thofe who Buy, are generally
far afunder, till the one Abating, and the
other Advancing, they agree at laft upon
the Price, fo it was very probable, that after the *Fœderato*'s had made their Demands,
the *Lillianians* would be more reafonable in
their Offers : Yet they did not as yet, go into fuch Lengths as to fay that a Peace even
upon thofe Terms, which the *Montalti* without Doors gave out, was preferable to a War,
tho' it afterwards prov'd they Thought fo
from the Conditions, they not only accepted, but gave Thanks for the Attainment of.

Not that there were altogether wanting
fome Deputies that dared to Efpoufe the finking Caufe of Liberty, and fpeak in Vindi-
cation of Alliances, which had been form'd
with the greateft Caution, and ought to
have been obferv'd with the greateft Re-

D   gard ;

gard: *Lecamero* took upon Him to fay the
Propofitions of the Enemy were *Infidious*,
and made on purpofe to put a ftop to the
Operations of the War, and *Regulo* a Patriot of the Equeftrian Order, difplay'd his
Eloquence in making it appear, that the
Grounds for a Treaty, ought to be of a
Peice, with the Reafons on which the War
was founded, and that the Preliminaries
before mention'd, were Captious, Infuffi-
cient, and Foreign to the Purpofe. It was
likewife urged by *Hamenio*, that the Con-
ferences ought to be broken up upon the
Lillianian Kings Refufal, to confent to more
equitable Conditions; and that Her Imperial Majefty fhould be requefted by the
Diet, to recal Her Legato's from the Place
of Treaty; tho' Strength of Argument was
oblig'd to give way to ftrength of Numbers,
and not only He, but all who fpoke on the
fame Side, had the Difatisfaction to fee the
Voice of Juftice and Reafon Silenced, by
the Clamours and Importunities of fuch as
were refolv'd to drop the Profecution of
the War at any Rate, fince its longer continuance would lay open thofe Intrigues,
and dark Defigns which nothing but a Fatal and Difhonourable Peace could keep
undifcover'd from the Publick Eye.

The Managers at *Helm* knew full well
that another Campaign would convince the
World,

World of the Facility of reducing the E-
nemy to what Terms it ſhould be thought
fitting to grant them, and they were appriz'd of what Diſſervice this Knowledge
would be to them and their Party, ſhould
it be Communicated to others by the Experience of freſh Conqueſts ; It was therefore
agreed amongſt themſelves to ſend Inſtructi-
ons to the *Mandarine Promato,* who was
put at the Head of their Armies in the Room
of the Glorious Prince *Mirabel,* to make
what Delays he could in the neceſſary Pre-
parations, and ſo to order his Affairs, that
the Legato who was his Collegue, and had
taken the Field with Reſolutions ſuitable
to his High Birth and Courage, ſhould fall
ſhort of accompliſh his Meaſures, which
were to bring the *Lillianians* to a Deciſive
Action, or break into the very Heart of
their Country, by opening himſelf a Paſſage
to it, by the Reduction of more Frontier
Towns. Theſe Orders to *Promato* who
was naturally of a daring and Enterprizing
Temper, were extremely Mortifying, and
thoſe that had contracted the cloſeſt Friend-
ſhip with Him, did not ſtick to ſay, that
at the Receipt of them he Repented of the
Acceptance of a Command that was ſo li-
mited, and ſubjected to ſuch ſevere Reflections : However, as he was *Paſſively*
Valiant from the Principles that were new-
ly taken up by his Maſters that had Pre-

fer'd

fer'd Him, as well as *Actively* refolute and
Couragious, fo he reprefs'd that Ardor that
pufh'd Him upon Hazardous Employments,
and did not join the above mention'd *Archon*, till the Enemy had alfo Encamp'd
themfelves, and had form'd themfelves into a Body of Forces capable of Facing thofe
of the *Federato*'s Army.

This Conjunction, tho' retarded by un-
neceffary Delays, was at laft made foon e-
nough to have determined the Fate of the
whole World, and to have freed it from
all further Apprehenfions of Exorbitant
Power, and the Effects of unmeafureable
Ambition, but when all things were got
ready for the Attack, when there wanted
nothing but the *Britomartians* confent to
fall on and Reap the Harveft of a moft
Glorious Conqueft, *Promato*, after many Excufes and Dilatory Artifices to put off a Declaration of his Opinion, upon his being
prefs'd by the *Archon* to go on to the Charge,
unwillingly made known to Him, that his
Orders with-held him from fuch an Attempt, and he had receiv'd pofitive Commands from Her Imperial Majefty, not to
run the Rifque of a Battle. Hereupon, he
was defired by his Collegue to be Affiftant
to him in Forming Two Important Sieges,
which would enable them to Penetrate
to the very Capital of all *Lilliania*, but in
this Point likewife he had no Power to Acquiefce,

quiefce, and returned for Anfwer, That
his Orders forbad him to enter upon any
Action whatfoever, either Battle or Siege.
So that all that the Brave and Undaunted
Archon, could fay to Him upon the Favourable Opportunity they had then put into
their Hands, of gaining an undoubted
Victory over the Enemy, and of forcing
them by that means to accept Laws, not
give them to the Conquerors, was in vain ;
tho' the faid *Archon* added the *Faderato's*
having pafs'd two Rivers, and Advanced
into the middle of the *Lillianian* Garrifons, could not then retire without the
Hazard of receiving a Blow, and that it
would have been better, if *Promato* had let
Him into the Knowledge of his Orders, before they approach'd fo near to the Enemies Army.

Luteolo had fometime before this, upon
Debates amongft the *Mandarines,* given his
Opinion, That tho' the Eafe and Tranquillity of the Empire was very defirable,
by reafon of the Preffures which his Fellow-Subjects labour'd under on Account of
the Expences of the War ; yet rather than
not carry it on till it could be brought to
a happy Period, he would joyfully content
himfelf with *Two Hundred Centenaries a*
Tear, which was not the Hundredth Part
of his Eftate: Young *Hamenio* had alfo
faid, upon the little Progrefs that was

made

made in giving the Finifhing Stroke to former Conquefts, that *The* Britomartians *were
making an unactive and a lazy Campaign, and
entring into a trifling Negotiation of Peace:
fo that they were amus'd by their Minifters at
Home, and trick'd by their Enemies abroad;*
which Expreffions had like to have coft him
his Liberty, and got him an Appartment in
the *Tulliano:* And now, upon this Occafion,
charg'd thofe with direct *Treachery,* that
had manag'd the Negotiations fo as to prevent Her Imperial Majefty's Troops from
acting in Concert with their Allies; to
this it was anfwer'd, by *Henrico,* that " it
" was not treacherous to manage Affairs
" for the Good and Advantage of the Em-
" pire, and that the Share he had in it,
" (for he was at the Bottom of the whole
" Project) tho' it was never fo much cen-
" fur'd, gave him the greateft Satisfac-
" tion imaginable: fo that he fhould think
" it a fufficient Recompence and Comfort
" to him all his Life, and he glory'd in
" it." What Reafon he had for fo doing
manifefted it felf only in the Intereft he
had amongft the *Proatins* (the Majority
of whom were too much influenc'd by
his Authority) which would have been
reckon'd of little Weight, had not he, as
it were, been the Fore-horfe of the Team
that forc'd the reft to draw after him.
The Allufion indeed is fomewhat courfe,

it

if apply'd to a Courtier, but ftill the
Comparifon will hold good amongft all
Lovers of Truth : And it was apparent,
that as *Novicius* play'd his Part with all
poffible Addrefs amongft the *Mandarines*,
by telling them, " That in the Peace
" which was then fet on foot, the Empire
" would find great Advantages to her felf,
" that it had never found any, or had any
" been ask'd for it in former Treaties :
" But that fuch things would be obtain'd
" for *Britomartia*, that fome of the Fœde-
" rato's would rather fee *Lilliania* poffefs'd
" of them ; and that thofe againft the Peace
" would have no reafon to complain, or be
" uneafy : fince the Terms were more ad-
" vantageous than they could wifh ;" So
did *Henrico* act his : Both of them making
Proteftations, that there was no feparate
Treaty, and that the fame would be *Foo-
lifh*, *Knavifh*, and *Villanous*. Which Declaration was defir'd by fome Members of
both Orders, to be obferv'd and remember'd.

And well did it deferve fuch a Notice as
was requefted to be taken of it ; for, after
the Diet had fallen foul upon *Delphino* in
a very virulent Charge, without making
any thing out againft him in a Court of
Judicature ; after they had given great
Sums for the carrying on the War in the
Kingdom of *Atalantis*, which fome of

them

them knew was by Confent to be abandon'd ; after they had out of Gratitude for
the Mercies of the Emperour *Aurantio*'s
Reign over them, reflected on his Memory, by endeavouring to take away (tho'
in vain) the Rewards he had given to his
Servants ; In a word, after they had loaded their beft Friends with the higheft
Indignities, and made their Court to their
worft Enemies ; after they had provided
for the Rich, that is *themfelves,* and fent
Thoufands of poor miferable Families,
that were before able to maintain themfelves by their honeft Labours a begging:
after they had difcountenanc'd Wit, and
laid heavy Impofts upon Learning, after
they had at random given it as their Opinion, that more Sums remain'd unaccoun-
ted for, than had almoft been given ; after
they had traduc'd the Living and defam'd
the Dead ; after they had broke thro' the
moft Sacred Engagements, and under the
Pretence of Religion, introduc'd a ftrange
Worfhip into one of the Provinces of the
Empire, they refolv'd to confide altogether in the Emprefs and her Minifters, and
leave it to them to act in Affairs of Peace
and War, which were the Prerogatives of
the Imperial Dignity, as fhould by them
be thought moft proper for, and conducive
to the Publick Welfare ; and retir'd from
the

the Pretorian-Hall for some Days, till *Palatina* should be at leisure to give them the Particulars of the Progress that had been made in the Treaty, which she had promis'd them from the Throne.

Expectation was upon the Rack, and every Day seem'd a Year till the Time was elaps'd to which the Diet had prefix'd their Meeting, as Hopes and Fears were alternately predominant ; and now, this bore the Ascendant over Mens Minds; and now, that took full Possession of them. A Peace was desirable to all Sorts and Conditions, but a Peace that had no Symptomes of Duration, that only skin'd over the Wounds of War, and left the Malady to break out with more Rage and Violence, was what was judg'd of the worst Consequence, and dreaded by such as made Reflections upon Consequences, and look'd into Futurity with the Eye of Reason and Thought. When the Day appointed for the Empress to impart to her People the Steps that had been made in the Negotiations, appear'd, and the Diet was told upon what Conditions a Peace might be had. The Terms were indeed advantageous to *Britomartia*, and many Concessions were made by the Enemy, that to all outward Appearance seem'd highly conducive to it's Wealth and Safety, but as the Interests of the Empire were so twisted and blended toge-

together with it's Neighbouring States and
Confederates, that without giving due Satisfaction to the others, it avail'd little or
nothing to her future Security to have a
feparate Agreement; fo thofe that had a
juft Senfe of Faith and Honour, and could
not without Abhorrence think of depar-
ting from the moft binding Alliances,
took upon them to difcover the Infincerity
of the Enemy, and to make appear, fince
the Kingdom of *Atalantis* was, by virtue
of the fore-going Articles, fuffer'd to remain in the Hands of the Ufurper; that
the Ends were no ways attain'd, for which
the *Fœderato*'s firft took Arms, and that they
could not with Honour to themfelves, or Juftice to the Powers whom they were engag'd
in Alliance with, lay them down till they
were fully and fatisfactorily accomplifh'd.

Amongft the Perfons that fpoke on this
fide were the *Mandarines Halfacio*, and
Æftivo, Two Nobles of unchangeable Sincerity, whofe Abilities were equal to their
Inclinations of doing Service to their
Country. The Firft with Strength of Reafon, Purity of Diction, and Cogency of
Argument, reprefented: " That tho' it
" was held confefs'd, that feveral Articles
" of the Treaty Entituled the Place of their
" Nativity to many feeming Advantages,
" yet what was therein ftipulated, would
" be of fhort Continuance without the mu-
" tual

" tual Guaranty of all the *Federato*'s for its
" Performance, and their reciprocal Se-
" curity. That the only means to engage
" every Member of the Alliance in such
" a Guaranty, was to procure for them
" equal Privileges with themselves, because
" their Pretensions were full as Just, espe-
" cially the *Allemannian*'s, which were
" infinitely greater : That the last of those
" Nations, tho' the War begun chiefly in
" Consideration of their violated Rights,
" seem'd wholly to be neglected, since
" they were allow'd only to keep Possessi-
" on of what they had already taken by
" Force of Arms, when they had an equi-
" table and fair Claim to the whole *Ata-*
" *lantick* Monarchy; and that the *Brito-*
" *martian* Faith by such a degenerate and
" causless Procedure, would in Time grow
" into a Proverb like the *Carthaginian*. The
last added to his Friends and Companions
Allegations (for they were inseperable from
each other, both in their Persons and Sentiments) by saying, " That the Measures
" enter'd into and pursued in *Britomartia*,
" for the Year last past, were contrary to
" Her Imperial Majesty's Engagements
" with Her Allies ; did Sully, and cast
" indelible Stains upon the Glories of a
" Reign that otherwise would have been
" Superlative in Lustre to all that had been
" before, or should come after it ; and would
" render

" render the *Britomartian* Name Odious to,
" and abhorr'd by every other Nation in
" the Univerfe. The Gallant Prince *Mirabel* fpoke to the fame Purpofe, and was Anfwer'd by the *Mandarine Temerario,* That *fome of their Allies would not fhew fuch a Backwardnefs to an Accommodation as they had lately manifefted, but for fome Members of that Illuftrious Affembly,* who maintain'd a Secret Correfpondence *with them, and endeavour'd to perfuade them to carry on the War, out of Confideration that there was a very ftrong Party in* Britomartia, *that in Procefs of Time would gain the Afcendant, and Cordially ftand by and fupport them, maugre all Oppofers.*

Now this *Temerario* had been appointed one of the Legato's, that brought the Negotiations Abroad to the Pofture they were then in, and had by the Haughtinefs of his Addrefs, made Himfelf fo unacceptible to the Perfons, who, he faid, were backward to come into the Treaty, that it was little wonder'd at, by thofe that had a true Infight into his Temper and Character, why he fhould fpeak without Book, and charge thofe with Clandeftine Practices, whom he could not prove to be Guilty of them. However, *Cupernico* condefcended to take notice of his Affertions ; and becaufe the *Mandarine Temerario,* had not exprefs'd Himfelf according to the Idiom of
the

the *Baitomartian* Tongue, took Occafion
from thence to fay ; " That, that Noble
" Perfon, had been fo long Abroad in Fo-
" reign Courts, that he had almoft for-
" got, not only the Language, but the
" Conftitution of his own Country. That
" according to the Laws of *Britomartia,*
" it could never be Suggefted as a Crime,
" in the meaneft Subject, much lefs in any
" Member of that Auguft Diet, *to hold*
" *Correfpondence with their Allies* : Such
" Allies efpecially whofe Intereft the Head
" of the Empire had declared to be I N-
" S E P E R A B L E from H E R O W N
" in Her Declaration from the Throne :
" Whereas, it would be a hard matter to
" juftifie, and reconcile with their Laws,
" or the Rules of Honour and Juftice,
" the Conduct of fome Perfons in Treat-
" ing *Clandeftinely* with the Common Ene-
" my, without the Participation of all the
" *Federato's.*

The next Article that fell under the *Mandarines* Cognizance, was that of the Advantages offer'd by the *Lillianians* relating
to Trade, particularly in fettling that
Branch of it, that more peculiarly belong'd to the Navigatorio, in the *Atalantick* and *Occidental* Sea. On this Occafion,
the Celebrated *Conde de Delphino,* than
whom none was better Vers'd in the *Ar-
cana's* of State affirm'd, That he did not
pretend

pretend to any great Knowledge in Matters of Traffick, but that during the time he had the Honour of being in the Administration of Affairs, he had obferv'd, and it was in his Power eafily to make it out from the *Contractorio* Books, that the fingle Commerce of *Porto Lufitano* brought to *Britomartia* in Times of War, doubly the Increafe of Wealth of the Trade to the Kingdom of *Atalantis* in Times of Peace: So that whatfoever might be infinuated to caft a Mift before the Eyes of the People, it was to be prefum'd, that the Traffick to *Atalantis* would ftill give leffer Productions, and fhorten in its Emoluments for the future, becaufe the *Lillianians* had made themfelves Abfolute and Uncontroulable Mafters of that large Extent of Dominions.

But after a long Debate, in which neither the above-mention'd Guarantee, nor the Confiderations of a more advantageous Traffick, which it was then in their Power to have eftablifh'd, had any manner of Prevalence, (tho' both of them had for their Advocates the Sage *Luteolo*, and the Perfuafive *Cupernico*) it was refolv'd to thank Her Imperial Majefty for communicating to the Diet the Conditions on which a Peace might be had, and to leave it to Her, and Her Miniftry's unerring Judgment and Difcretion, fo to go on with thofe
Tranf-

Tranfactions, and in fuch a manner to pursue what they had fo happily begun, as they in their great Wifdom fhould think fit.

Yet, tho', upon putting it to the Vote whether they fhould acquiefce under the Empreffes wife Determinations for the Advantage of the People, it was carry'd in the Affirmative by a very great Majority; there were not wanting feveral Men of Diftinction amongft the *Mandarines,* who to hand themfelves down with unblemifh'd, and untainted Characters to Pofterity, enter'd their Diffatisfaction againft fuch Proceedings, and their Reafons for difagreeing with thofe that had the right Side of the Queftion, tho' the wrong Side of the Argument. Hiftory gives us their Remonftrance at large, which was as juftifiable in the Compofure of it, as it was allowable from immemorial Precedents of the fame Nature, in its being inferted in the Minutes of the Diet; but fince this prefent Undertaking, is to give a fuccinct and fhort Account of Tranfactions; it is purpofely omitted and left out for the fake of Brevity; tho' the Reader is to be told, That what Juftice foever might appear on its Side, and from whatfoever Exemplars in the Journals of the Diet it might be taken, it gave fuch Offence, and exafperated thofe that had no Relifh for it fo very
much,

much, that it was order'd to be erafed out of their Journals, and thereby difcountenanc'd from getting into the Approbation of thofe that fat up for Judges of Political Tranfactions without Doors.

However the Subftance of it was made publick, in order to let the Populace into the Reafons upon which they grounded their Diffent, which was fo ill taken by the Favourite Party, that they apply'd to the Throne to iffue out a Reward for the Difcovery of the Authors of that Contrivance, after they had in vain made Enquiries relating to that Subject among themfelves. This was readily affented to, and an Edict was given out, according to the Tenour of their Petition; tho' it was whifper'd, not without Reafon, that they might more readily have attain'd to the Knowledg of what they were in queft of, had they fearch'd more narrowly amongft themfelves, or been appriz'd of any particular Inftance where any one of their own Members had been animadverted upon for fuch an allowable and harmlefs a Publication.

'Twas obfervable alfo, that even amongft the *Proatins*, the generality of them were at firft ftartled and ftrangely furpriz'd, at the Propofitions which were likewife communicated to them. They had promis'd themfelves Mountains from the Affurances,

that

that had been given them by the Minifters
of their own Order, and now were under
a Neceffity of holding themfelves conten-
ted with Mole-Hills, becaufe they could
not go back from their Engagements, or
depart from that implicite Affent they were
oblig'd to give every Scheme that was handed down to them from the Court. However fome of them made no Scruple of de-
claring, That it was eafy to difcern what
Reafons induc'd thofe who fat at Helm,
to keep the Refult of the Negotiations between *Britomartia* and the *Lillianians* fo
long while a Secret ; fince, if fuch a Plan,
as was then laid before them, had been
communicated to the Diet, before a Majority had been fecur'd, and the Minds of
the Deputies prepar'd by a long Train of
artful Infinuations to receive it ; it would,
in all probability, have been unanimoufly
exploded. But by the admirable Dexte-
rity of the Prime Minifters, Things were
brought to fuch a Pafs, that tho' amongft
the *Proatins* One or Two Members open'd
their Mouths, to propofe taking the important Matters that had been imparted to
them into their immediate Confiderations
they were prefently ftopp'd by a General
Cry, for paying their Acknowledgments to
the Emprefs *Palatina*, and expreffing their
Satisfaction in what Her Majefty had al-

E   ready

ready done, and their *entire Confidence*, in
Her Majefty's continuing to purfue the
true Intereft of her Imperial Territories.

Yet notwithftanding, the vaft difpropor-
tion of Numbers between fuch as went into the Meafures which were then taken,
and fuch as judg'd them difadvantagious
and unreafonable, *Hamenio* was too good
a Patriot, not to make a ftand once more
againft the Torrent, that was breaking
in upon the Liberties of Mankind, and to
dehort them from laying hold of too rafh
Expedients, under the Pretence of Ways
and Means for the Common Benefit. " I
" am but too fenfible, *faid he*, that what
" I am now going to fpeak, will have as
" little Influence upon this Affembly, as
" what has been already fpoken by me and
" other Well-wifhers to the Conftitutions
" of the Empire; Yet tho' Men that are Re-
" folv'd to be deaf, will give not Ear to
" the Voice of Truth and Reafon, be they
" never fo open and apparent: Tho' I ex-
" pect Reproaches and a Calumnious
" Treatment, for giving an Opinion which
" my Compaffion for our felves and others,
" my concern for the Liberties of the whole
" Univerfe, and the Love I bear to our moft
" Excellent Conftitution dictate to me, I
" can't even now but make it my endeavour
" to lay before you the Evil Confequences
" of

" of what you are now going to do, by ap-
" plauding fuch Conditions of Agreement
" with the Common Enemy, as muft in-
" fallibly terminate andConclude (after the
" Cement of a moft Solid Alliance is there-
" by disjoin'd and unloos'd,) in the Ruin of
" every particular State and Principality
" that forms it. I do not this, *Gentlemen*,
" in hopes of your Conviction, for I know
" what Odds the moft wholefome and beft
" Advice has at this time of Day againft
" it ; but I do this to Acquit my felf be-
" fore Angels and Men of the Guilt, I muft
" otherwife be fharer in. 'Tis too late,
" indeed, to recal the Vote that has been
" made and agreed unto, 'Tis to late to
" tell you, that the Gifts the Enemy has
" made, are like thofe from the *Greeks* to
" the *Trojans* in Order to Deftroy us :
" 'Tis too late to affirm that the Places
" which are to be Surrendred into your
" Hands by this Treaty, will but ferve as
" fo many Garrifons to keep up a ftand-
" ing Army in Times of Peace, fince you
" have not only accepted of them, but have
" been Lavifh of your Thanks, for having
" it in your Power to give them your Ac-
" ceptance : But it is not to late, (tho' e-
" ven this Opportunity if now loft may be
" paft Retreiving) fo to provide for the
" fafety of the Empire, that the Succeffion

to

" to the Imperial Diadem, as far as in Us
" lies may be fecured, by more ample De-
" clarations in its Favour, and that all the
" Potentates engag'd in the Prefent War
" againft *Lilliania*, may be defired to vin-
" dicate and affert the feveral *Decreto's*
" that have been made for that Purpofe,
" and jointly take Arms againft all fuch as
" fhall endeavour to make void that Efta-
" blifhment : Since the beft of Princes are
" fubject to the Laws of Mortality, and
" even *Palatina* Herfelf muft one Day,
" (which I pray may be far, very far di-
" diftant) exchange the Glories of this
" Earthly Life, to be crown'd with the
" Bleffings of that which is Heavenly.

Endeavours were us'd to have this puz-
zling Motion dropp'd, but *Hamenio* and
fome of his Friends infifting to have it propos'd to the Diet ; it was carry'd in the
Negative almoft unanimoufly, and gave
Birth to a Refolution of a quite different
Nature, which imported, That the Diet
had fuch an entire Relyance upon the Affurances the Emprefs *Palatina* had given
them, relating to the Security of the Succeffion to the Throne after Her Deceafe,
that they could never doubt of Her Imperial Majefty's taking proper Meafures for it ;
and that they would befeech Her Majefty to
dif-

difcountenance all thofe who fhould endeavour to raife Jealoufies between Her
and Her Subjects, efpecially by mifrepre-
fenting Her Intentions. This Requeft had
an Anfwer to the Satisfaction of thofe that
made it, and many zealous Oppugners of
Invafions upon the Rights and Immunities
that had been feemingly fecur'd to them
by inviolable Decreto's, had the Mortification to be convinc'd, that if a Motion of
fo great Importance and Neceffity could
not meet with a favourable Reception;
they could have but little Hopes of accom-
plifhing Defires of lefs Weight and Moment.

What remain'd for the *Diet* to do, now
the Time generally allotted for their Sitting
was almoft Elaps'd, was to Arm themfelves againft the Invectives they had
Grounds to expect from an Enrag'd Populace, whom they at their feveral Elections
had gain'd over into a Belief of being releas'd from all further Impofts and Subfidies, after the Finifhing of that one Seffion. They were Confcious to themfelves
how little they had kept their Word with
them, and apprehenfive, left the *Literato's*,
whom they had mightily Exafperated, by
laying a Duty upon the Barks of Trees, on
which all their ufeful Panegyricks and Sa-

E 3   tyrs

tyrs were pen'd down, nnd their Historical Remarks and Observations transmit-
ted to Posterity, should make them Returns
suitable to their Merits, and set forth the
great Discouragement they had given, not
only to the Products of the Brain, but the
Manufactures of the Soil to which they ow'd
their Nativity. It had always been among
the other Privileges of the *Britomartian* Empire, that the Subject, who thro' the mean-
ess of his Condition, or his want of Interest
amongst the Great Men, who surrounded
the Throne, and intercepted the Beams of
Majesty, from shining more immediately
upon those that stood in need of the Rays
of its Protection, could not apply in Person
for Redress of Grievances, should Commu-
nicate them to the Publick in Writing, that
so, by those Means, the Sovereign, among
such as were curious in Enquiries of that
Nature, might be let into the Knowledge
of them. This Method had often been of
great Help to the Oppressed, and made
the Empress appriz'd of several Male-
Practices, which She had never known but
by the Means of it; and this had been so
useful in propagating the New Scheme,
that the Old one had still continu'd in
Force, but for the Exercise of it. Therefore, to express their Gratitude to an *Art*
to which their Elevation to the Dignities
they

they were poffefs'd of, it was judg'd re-
quifite, leaft the Artillery that play'd fo
fuccefsful on their Side fhould be turn'd
againft them, wholly to difmount it and
nail it up.

What gave Occafion to this unpreceden-
ted Refolution, was, the Publication of a
certain Remonftrance, that was voted a
Libel for being unanfwerable, and faid to
be an Infult againft the Supreme Authority, only for imploring, with all Humi-
lity, its Aid and Affiftance : and what
pufh'd them on to form that Refolution
into a Decreto was fomething of the fame
Nature done by one of the Prime Sacrifto's, who could not fee the moft approv'd
Fidelity fet at nought, the moft exalted Worth fcandaliz'd and deprefs'd, the
moft inimitable Fortitude cowardiz'd and
calumniated, without an Exclamation in
Behalf of thofe Virtues, without fome Tokens of Diffatisfaction for the Injury that
was done to fuch Heroick and Shining
Qualities.

Even thofe Sacred Pages had not ftrength
and Energy enough to defend them from
the rude and Importunate Affaults of Cla-
morous

morours Tongues. The Doctrines that
were in them taught ; and the Eftablifh'd
Truth that were in them bravely Vindica-
ted, were forc'd to give way to falfe Suggeftions, and fubmit to the partial Decifion of
our unjuft Cenfure; as that which was Holy, that which was Loyal, that which had
no Views in it but Reproof and Inftructions,
underwent the Reproach of being otherwife
intended, and the Meek, the Learned, the
Couragious *Dafavia*, for daring to lament
the Vices of a corrupt and degenerate
Age, was accus'd and declar'd guilty of
endeavouring to create Difcord and Sedi-
tion in the Heart of the Empire.

So Bold a Stroke as this, againft a Perfon of his Title and Character, could not
but be the Subject of various Speculati-
ons, and Men who thought clofely, and
made enquiry into the Confequences of
violent and precipitate Meafures were
taught by Experience, that the Goodnefs
of a Caufe was fhrewdly to be fufpected,
when it was carried on and Supported by
Acts of Intemperance and Rigour. Therefore inftead of gaining Profelytes over to
their Opinion, they loft many of their former Adherents, who being engag'd on
their fide by fpecious Pretences, deferted
them

them when it appear'd, that thofe Pretences were nothing elfe but mere Delufions; and the Unadvifed *Montalti* had the Mortification to fee, that tho' they increas'd in Number within Doors, thro' the means of an Invifible Power, which Places of Profit will always be poffefs'd of, they decreas'd daily without.

They knew and were fully fatisfied, that if their Intereft fell off and abated in fuch a manner while they were Sitting, the Defection would be much greater when the Awe and Authority of their Prefence fhould be remov'd, and they difpatch'd Home to look after their Domeftick Affairs in their feveral Habitations; They knew that the Tongues and Pens of Men wonld be Exercifed freely, with Refpect to the Iffue of their Confultations and Debates, after their Rifing, and fince it had been Cuftomary at the Clofe of every *Diet*, for the People to be entertain'd with the True, and falfe Steps that had been made in it, either to Excite their Refentment or provoke their Applaufe, it was but too vifible, the fame Meafures would be taken in Relation to their Proceedings.

Wherefore

Wherefore they took it inftantly into their Confideration, how to ftiffle all Attempts of that kind; and becaufe they were confcious to themfelves, that the Licenfe which had Time out of Mind been given to the Practice above mention'd, might be employ'd to their Difadvantage, they enter'd upon Vigorous Efforts wholly to Supprefs it. But as this Liberty of Publifhing Mens Thoughts of the Conduct of their Superiors, had been equally Abus'd on the one fide and the other, and both Diftinctions of Parties had made ufe of it as a Vehicle, in which they convey'd their Complaints, in order to obtain Remedies for theDifafters that griev'd them; fo, that the Intended Decreto might bear fome Colour of Juftice, and wear' the Face of Impartiality, it was gravely declared, that no *Anonymous* Writer fhould dare to Iffue forth the Labours of his Brain under the fevereft Penalty. Not, but it was wifely forefeen by the Oppofite Party, that this Pretended Act of Impartiality, was defign'd altogether in favour of the *Montalti* Perfuafion, fince they had in fuch a manner engrofs'd the Adminiftration of Affairs to themfelves, that it was not only in their Power to Animadvert upon, and Punifh whomfoever they fhould be pleas'd to Call Offenders,

but

but to pass by, releafe, and acquit such as really fell under the Cognizance of the Law, and justly Merited the Names of Common Defamers.

Several Flagrant instances of this Method of Procedure were seen, during their very Confultations upon this Head ; and even the Refolutions they had taken to provide againft the growing Evil of Detraction were ufher'd into the World with Tokens of its Approbation, and Increafe. This great and good Man that liv'd up to the Rules of Honour and Honefty, and never fwerv'd from the Dictates of an Untainted Confcience, was Bawled about the Streets, for one that was void of Shame and Integrity, and every Embellifhment that gave a Luftre to his Character. That Valiant and Unconquer'd General, which never turn'd his Back upon a Foe, nor ever look'd an Enemy in the Face, whom he did not put to Flight ; that never did one fingle Act in Difobedience to his Sovereign, or committed any Thing in Violation of his Love to his Country, by way of Return to his paft Services was called a Robber, a Daftard, an Ingate, and faid to be almoft Emafculated, to pleafe fuch as were Envious of his great Abilities. In a Word, it avail'd nothing in Behalf of the moft Confum-

mate

mate Faith and Experience, that they were
Superlative to all Imitation; and the moſt
Tranſcendent Merit had nothing to comfort itſelf with, under its Ignominious
Treatment, but the Want of it, in ſuch as
decryed and reviled it; while thoſe that
were actually at Work, in providing a-
gainſt Infamy and Scandal, Laugh'd behind the Curtain at the Progreſs of it;
nay, what is more, if the Annals of Time
ſpeak true, Encourag'd, and Rewarded ſuch
as gave vent to it.

But with whatſoever Application and
Warmth they ſtudy'd to prevent the Inſults
they were threaten'd with, and to divert
the Storm that was coming upon them
with their approaching Diſmiſſion, it unhappily fell out that their Uneaſineſs at the
Remonſtrances of a Neighbouring State,
ſummon'd all their Reſentments that way,
and hurry'd them into ſuch Extremities of
Anger, that to take their full Revenge on
the Laſt, they dropp'd the Purſuit of the
Firſt; and, (to the great Grief of the Syn-
dyke *Eborocano*, who amidſt all his Want
of Inſight into Things and Men, very
luckily knew his own Blindſide; and that
he was as liable, as any Man breathing,

(77)

to the Attacks of that Derifion and Satyr which he had labour'd with all his Might to filence) left that Affair in the fame Condition they found it.

So that after both Orders of this General Diet had fignaliz'd themfelves in making Provifion to fupply the Expences of a War, while they had nothing more in View than an approaching Peace; after the one had confented to all the Funds which the other propos'd, and the *Mandarines* were at laft brought to comply and go hand in hand with the *Proatins*: After they had receiv'd Subftantial Proofs of Gratitude from thofe who fat at Helm, in Places of Honour and Profit, and gracious Affurances of the moft obliging Remembrances from the Emprefs; they had leave to return from the Pretorian-Hall with *PALATINA*'s Thanks, to their refpective Places of abode, there to go without the Thanks of their Country; there to contemplate upon the Benefits they had promis'd to their feveral Electors; and to furnifh themfelves with Excufes for the Breach of thofe Ways and Means in order to make new Affurances.

Thus

Thus ended the Debates of an Affembly, whofe Memory was afcertain'd of
being tranfinitted and convey'd to the
lateft Ages, through the Means of the
moft remarkable Occurrences ; Thus was
a Refpite given to the Exercife of that
Authority, which as it ow'd its Inftitution
to the Breath of the Sovereign, and the
People, fhould alone have confulted their
refpective Honour and Advantage; and
thus did they for a while ceafe to load
the *Britomartians* with frefh Impofts, who
were chofen on purpofe to releafe from
them the heavy Burthen of their Debts, and
other National Grievances: Which how
they perform'd has been made appear in
the Courfe of the foregoing Hiftory, that
has told the Reader fome Particulars,
which the Author could have wifh'd had
never happen'd. Since, how remote foever
the Age they were tranfacted in, is from
that which we now live in; it is but too
well known, by fatal Experience, that paft
Examples of all forts of Tendency, as well
bad as good, have had their Influence upon fucceeding Times.

F I N I S.

The
Adventures
of Five Englishmen
from
Pulo Condoro

by

Walter Vaughan

Bibliographical note:

*This facsimile has been made from a copy in the
Beinecke Library of Yale University
(British Tracts 1714 V46)*

THE
ADVENTURES
OF
Five Englishmen
FROM
Pulo Condoro.

THE
ADVENTURES
OF
Five Englishmen
FROM
Pulo Condoro,
A Factory of the New Company in the
EAST-INDIES.

Who were Shipwreckt upon the little Kingdom of Jehore, not far diftant, and being feized on by the Inhabitants, were brought before the King, and detain'd for fome Months; With the many Accidents that befel them during their Abode in that Ifland

Together with an Account of the Mannors and Cuftoms of the Inhabitants, and of the Birds, Beafts, Fruits, &c. both of the Iflands of Jehore, and Pulo Condore:

Written by Mr. *Vaughan,* One of the Adventurers.

LONDON: Printed for *C. Bates,* at the *Sun* and *Bible,* in *Pye Corner* ; and *A. Bettefworth,* at the *Red-Lion* on *London-Bridge.* 1714.

THE
ADVENTURES
OF
Five Englishmen
FROM
Pulo Condora, &c.

UPON the 9th of
this Inftant, Cap-
tain *Rachell*, the
Chief of the Factors of *Pulo
Condore*, Mr. *Williams*, Secretary, and Mr. *George Bright*,
Steward, with Captain *Chefton* and my felf, all came on

Anno
170⅔.
Jan. 19.

B 2   Board

Board the Ship *Safeguard* in a
small Prow belonging to the
Natives of the Island from
Factory Bay, which is on
the *South-East* Part of the
largest Island, on Board the
Ship riding in *Pulc Condore*
Harbour. This Harbour is
made by an Inlet between the
Two greatest Islands, and
lyes *N. W.* by *N.* and *S. E.*
by *S.* which is your Course
in. The best Anchoring is
about Two Cables length off
Shore of the Southmost Bay
on the least Island, where you
have the Bay fair open, and
you have Six or Seven Fa-
thom Water. Now the same
Prow had Four Guns put into her, each near a Thou-
sand Weight, Seven Huddles
Six Foot broad, and Fifteen
Foot long, a Butt of Lime,

a

a Canister of Sugar, a Musket, Cartouch Box, Four Gun Cartridges, a Case Bottle of fresh Water, and about Fourteen Gallons of Rack, the She Cat, and her Two Young Ones, which belonged to the Two Women. After Nine or Ten Days Stay in the said Harbour for a favourable Opportunity to go to the Factory, on the 18th of *January* imbark'd on the Prow with Mr. *Williams*, Mr. *Bright*, and my self, (*Vaughan*) with Four lent Men belonging to the said Ship, with the Smith's Wife, and her Young Child, Born on the said Island. The said Mr. *Bright* having the Charge of the Boat, went to rowing to get through the Gut between the Two Islands; just as we en-

B 3　　tred

Anno
170⅔. tred the Gut the Ship made
a weft with her Enfign, and
fired a Gun, (a Signal for us
to return) which was an-
fwered by our making for
the Ship again ; but the Ship-
boat rowing and waving to
us, we lay on our Oars till
fhe came Aboard. *Mr. Williams*, *Bright*, *Vaughan*, and
Packet, and the Woman, went
Aboard the Pinnace, and
left *Edward Bethall* and *John
Bremeridge* in the Prow at
Anchor between the Ship
and the Gut. When they came
Aboard the Ship Captain
Chefton began to Scold at Mr.
Bright, asking, whether he
had not been there long e-
nough to know the Place,
and fee when Squalls threatned themfelves from the
Hills? Adding, that if the
Boat

Boat were his he would not
venture her in his Charge;
and that if we were once but
a Ship's length to Leeward
of the Gut, 'twould be im-
poffible for the Prow e'er to
fetch in again.

This Morning the Wo-
man told the Captain, that
they had been troubled in
the Night with ftrange and
frightful Dreams, as did
likewife Mr. *Williams*, the
Clerk of the Factory; that
their Hearts fail'd them; and
that they had rather undergo
the Fatigue of travelling o'er
the Hills, and through the
Woods, than venture about
with the Prow. This Morn-
ing as I was Smoaking a Pipe
in the Larboard Gang-way
my Nofe dropp'd Six or Seven Drops of Blood on my

The 19h.

B 4　　Hand,

Hand, Captain *Rachell*'s Son
feeing it, ask'd what was the
Matter? What made my
Nofe Bleed? And immediately went and told Captain
Chefton of it, who fent for
me, and ask'd me, what made
my Nofe Bleed? I told him
I could not tell, and that it
was not ufual; whereupon he
told me, if my Heart mif-
gave me I need not go, that
he would order another in
my Room. I told him I
was not at all fearful, tho'
moft of our People were:
One faying he would not
venture his old Shoes, another, that he would not go,
though ordered; in fhort,
not one among them thought
fhe would get fafe about.
This Day about Three *P. M.*
the Weather promifing fair,
we

we rowed through the Gut,
and having a moderate turning Gale, fet our Sail, and
ftood off from the Ifland
pretty far, in hopes on the
next Tack to fetch a fmall
Ifland that lyes a little to the
Weftward of the Weftmoft
Point, which firft opens the
Bay; but on the contrary,
when we tack'd and ftood
for the Shore, fudden and
hard Gales of Wind came off
from the Land upon us,
which forc'd us to fhorten
our Sail, and heave the Hur-
dles Over-board, which lying very high, forc'd us very
faft to Leeward, upon which
we came to Anchor to Lee-
ward of the Gut, which runs
into the Harbour, and there
rid till Two *P. M.* next Day,
the force of Wind ftill con-
B 5   tinuing,

Anno
170¾.   tinuing, and forcing in fo
much Water, the Prow be-
ing Leaky withal, that we
could hardly keep her free
with our utmoft Endeavours,
which with the Violence of
the Waves put us every Mi-
nute in fearful Expectations
of the Boat's parting, fhe having not fo much as one
Timber, and her Planks being fewed together.

The 20th.   This 21 Hours we have
had hard Gales of Wind, attended with fudden and hard
Squalls off Land ; about Two
this Afternoon we weigh'd,
intending to Row nigher
the Shore into a fmall opening of Land, in hopes that
there we fhould have found
fmoother Water, and more.
Shelter from the Wind ; we
got in, but found the Water
no

no smoother, the Wind not
a whit less violent, nor any
possibility of getting ashore,
by reason of the dangerous
Rocks and excessive Break-
ers, wherewith it was lined ;
but having with extream,
and almost unsuccessful Fatigue, got clear of the big-
est and outermost Rock, we
let go our Anchor in about
Seven Fathom Water, with
both ends of the Cable bent
to it, because the outer end,
before bent, was stranded
about 30 Fathoms from the
Clinch ; we veer'd what
scope we could, but to little
Purpose ; for the violent
Gusts of Wind which from
the Land pour'd their utmost
Fury upon us, and the Moun-
tain-like Seas, drove us from
our Anchor-hold at so great

a

a rate, that we were in a short time obliged to hawl it up. Being now Adrift, we set our Sail Half-maft high, endeavouring, if poffible, to keep her Head to the Wind ; but fo great was the Sea which tofs'd us before it, and fo irrefiftible the Wind, that our almoft finking Boat could not hold up her Sides: Great, but fruitlefs, were our Endeavours to heave out the Water fafter than it came in, which, with being quite Spent, we (with what Reluctance foever) were forc'd to commit our weak Boat to the Mercy of mercilefs Winds and raging Waves, and our felves to the immediate Protection of our moft Merciful and Compaffionate Creator , without which

which it had been Stupidity
to think of furviving thofe
difmal impending Dangers
in fo crazy and leaky a Boat.
The difmal Idea with which
every rowling Sea reprefented Death to us was height-
ned by the fad Moans made
among our felves : And certainly our Extremity was as
great as any thing finite
could be capable of ; no
Danger could be greater,
none nearer than that of
Drowning ; or if by Mira-
cle we efcap'd that, from
what lefs than Omnipotence
cou'd we expect Subfiftence,
without any thing to Eat or
to Drink ? Or where could
we think of going without
a Compafs, or any other Inftrument to help or guide us
in this our great Diftrefs ?
                    This

This Night having quite worn out what we before ufed to Bale out the Water, we ftav'd in one Head of a Six Gallon Cask of Rack for that Ufe, out of which we filled a Five Pint Bottle, and a *China* Bowl, holding near Two Quarts ; they that were fo minded taking a Dram of the remains before it was thrown away.

The 21ft. Finding that the Gale, though ftill very hard, and the Seas very great, was grown more fteddy, we again ventured to hoift our Sail Half-maft up, and fteer'd as near as we could guefs a *S. W.* Courfe. This Morning we hove over-board the Four Gun-Cartridges, and the Butt of Lime, to lighten the Boat ; about Eleven *P. M.* fome

some of us looking in the
bundle of Child's Clouts we
had in the Boat, found Five
small White Biskets, which
(though as soft as Pap with
Salt Water) went down very
cordially; and for which we
return'd Thanks to Almighty God, faithfully promising,
that if it were his Blessed
Will to Preserve our Lives
in this great Exigence, that
we would never forget his
great Mercy; and that we
would put Bills into all Christian Churches, desiring the
Congregations to join with
us in giving God Almighty
Thanks for his so great De-
liverance. It was now Three
Days since any of us had Eat
any thing, by which we were
become so weak, that *John
Bremeridge* was heaving the
Water

Water out of the Boat, a-
bout Midnight the Sea over-
took us, and (the Boat not
rifing fo lively as fhe fhould)
ftruck the Cag out of his
Hand, which obliged us to
go to our laft Shift, the Eight
Gallon Cag: If that through
any Misfortune fhould Stave,
or go Over-board, we muft
neceffarily Sink, for we had
nothing elfe wherewith we
could Bale. The Rack we
emptied into an Iron-bound
Wafhing-Tub, belonging to
a Woman at *Pulo Condore*,
but in lefs than Three Hours
it was fill'd up by the Spray
of the Sea, and was fpoil'd,
as was likewife the Canifter
of Sugar half through. Our
Courfe I judge to be *Weft*,
Diftance 50 Miles from the
Ifland.

A

A conftant ftill Gale, and
a great hollow Sea continued ; this Morning as we
were heaving out the Water,
we found a fmall Fifh, which
by Confent we gave to the
Cat and her Two Young
Ones, defigning to Eat them ;
but our Stomachs fail'd us,
and our Cries were only for
Water to quench our Thirfts,
which were increas'd through
our want of fomething to
Shade us from the Sun by
Day, and the Dews by Night.
Courfe by Eftimation *S. W.*
Diftance 120 Miles.

The firft Part of thefe 24
Hours the Wind and Sea
much the fame as Yefterday,
but the latter Part we found
both lefs Wind, and the Sea
much abated, which encou-
raged us to hoift up our Sail
atrip,

Anno
170 $\frac{2}{7}$.
The 22d.

The 23d.

Anno
170⅖.

The 24th.

atrip, the Prow seeming to
fly through the Water. Courfe
per Judgment *W. S. W.* and
S. W. by *W.* Diftance 130.

Fine Weather, and indifferent fmooth Water; at Three
P. M. we faw Three fmall I-
flands, diftant about 15′; at
Sun-fet we Anchored in a
fmall Bay on the *W.* Side of
the largeft, in Sight of the
MainLand. Courfe fince Noon
S. W. by *W* Diftance 18′.

There went afhore *Edward
Bethall* and my felf in fearch
of frefh Water, but could not
find any; we faw an Image of
a Man cut out in Wood, a-
bout Two Foot high, and
this was all the Signs we
could fee of any Body's ever
having been here; we faw
great ftore of Fifh, but had
not any thing wherewith to
take

take any. About Seven *P. M.*
we weigh'd, and ftood for
the Main with a frefh Gale,
but no great Sea.

At Two *P. M.* our Rud-
der or Commodity broke,
and was loft, notwithftanding withal at Seven *Ditto* we
came to an Anchor fairly in
with the Shore, under a very Remarkable Bluff Head of
Land, where we rid all Night ;
at break of Day we weighed
and row'd about the Head-
land, where we found a River, into which we row'd ;
it had a Bar at the Mouth of
it, though no great Sea ; the
beft Paffage over it is on the
Eaftmoft Side, where there
is Water enough for large
Veffels to go over at half
Flood ; about Nine this
Morning we laid our Boat
　　　　　　　　　afhore

aſhore on the Side of a ſteep
Sand, and *Edward Bethall* and
my ſelf went again aſhore on
queſt of freſh Water, which
to the great Satisfaction of
us all we found Plenty and
Good, and got ſome Shell-
fiſh; and had we had a Hat-
chet or large Knife we might
have made a Rudder; we
ſaw no People, but found a
large Tree half made into a
Canoe, the Tracks of ſeveral
Wild Beaſts, and ſeveral Places where Fires had been
made, a little Houſe made
with Rattans, and hung on
a Tree almoſt a-breaſt of our
Prow where ſhe lay; and in
a ſmall Bay were erected
Spars after the manner of a
China Fiſhing Ware. This
was a very large and deep River, running between plea-
ſant

sant Banks, adorn'd with
strait and tall Trees : We
made a Fire, and staid here
to Refresh our selves all this
Day and Night.

We in the Night conclu-
ded to go up the River, but
our Hearts failing, in the
Morning we agreed to go
out again, we having heard
that what People liv'd herea-
bouts were Savage, Cruel
People ; we knew that they
had little or no Commerce
with any *Europeans*, and by
consequence we might ex-
pect they shou'd be the less
civilliz'd. We found a beaten Path from out of the
Woods to the Place where
we got our fresh Water, but
whether made by Men, or
Wild Beasts, God knows ;
we likewise found a Paddle
made

Anno
170$\frac{2}{7}$.

made in the Form in the Margent, and several Heaps of Oister-shells ; where we found these, we likewise found there had been Fires made ; in the Evening we all heard what was both Pleasant and Surprizing, *viz.* Birds, that in their Notes exactly imitated the Ringing of Five Bells in *England*, both very loud and very shrill : Our Sleep in the Boat has been undisturbed by any Noises whatever. Having fill'd the Tub with Sand, we gathered up what dry Wood we could light of, that we might carry Fire with us, (for we had lost the Flint of our Piece) and filled the Case-Bottle and *China* Bowl with fresh Water ; according to our last Resolution we

we row'd out of the River,
reeft and shifted our Sail,
in order to Sail Stern fore-
most, that we might Steer
with an Oar on each Side ;
for her Stern was so high that
an Oar would not have
reach'd the Water ; (it fell
out very happily for us that
the Rudder did not break
during the bad Weather.
These Rudders or Commo-
dities are very near Two
Thirds the length of the
Prow, and when slipt, reach
almost half way under her
Bottom ;) we steer'd along
Shore, which was indifferent
low Land, beset with strait
and tall Trees, and at Night
Anchored before a large River's Mouth, which seem'd
a Fine large River, on the
Eastmost Side of which we
saw

Anno
170⅔.

saw a great Fire almoft all Night. The 24 Hours fair Weather, moderate Gales, and fmooth Water.

The 27th.

At Day-break we weigh'd, coafting along Shore ; about Ten this Forenoon *John Bre-meridge* took a Booby, which we fhared among us, and Eat as contentedly as if it had been the moft delicious Fare ; it had on it about as much Meat as a fmall lean Pigeon. Fair Weather, fmooth Water ; at Night we anchored about Two Miles from the Shore ; it is very low Land.

The 28th.

At Five this Morning we made a Sail, ftanding along Shore with a brisk Gale of Wind ; at Eight *A.M* paft by a River, and at Eleven faw a great Fire on the Shore ; we

we were fomething minded Anno 170¾.
to ftand toward the Shore,
but it pleafed God to alter
our Refolution, by putting
us in hopes that in Two
or Three Days we fhou'd either reach the Streights of
Sincapore, or luckily fee a
Ship, this being the Time of
Year that they come from
the Coaft of *China:* This
Afternoon we faw Three
Iflands to Windward of us,
and the Main Land trench-
ing to the Windward like-
wife, fhewing itfelf like broken Land, infected with
Rocks in many Parts of it. At
Four *P. M.* we betook our
felves to Rowing, in hopes to
have gain'd the headmoft
Ifland, but were grown too
weak to hold out through
our want of Food, and con-
            B   ftant

ſtant Fatigue of heaving out the Water; and it was impoſſible to turn to Windward, having loſt our Rudder, ſo was forc'd to Anchor in a Bay on the Lee Shore. *Note*, That *Nathaniel Packet* has lain like a Dead Man ever ſince we left the firſt Iſlands we made, ſaying, he had loſt the Uſe of his Limbs.

At Ten *A. M.* we weigh'd with fair Weather, and a brisk Gale of Wind; Three of us, (the Fourth being employed to heave out the Water) endeavour'd to Row to the Leewardmoſt Iſland, but found that though we pull'd with the utmoſt of our Strength, yet it avail'd nothing, ſo weak were we grown for want of Food.

Find-

Finding we made no Hand with Rowing, we a-
greed to go Ashore, tho' on
the Sand we could see neither
wild Hogs or Tigers ; so miferable was our Condition,
that we were forc'd to truft
to the Mercy of the Wild
Beafts, (or for what
we knew) as Wild Men ;
one or t'other we expected,
but could no longer abide in
the Boat, so drove towards
the Shore till so nigh that
we judged the Cable would
reach the Shore, then dropt
Anchor, and Veer'd away,
that being the only Way to
get fafe Ashore, the Surf was
so great: But notwithftanding the Care we took, feveral Seas broke clear over the
Boat, the firft of which
drowned the Two Young
B 2   Kittens,

Kittens, but the old Cat
saved her self by nimbly. getting up to the Maſt Head;
nor was ſhe leſs nimble in
getting down again when
we call'd her, by which
Means ſhe got ſafe Aſhore
with us ; we carried Aſhore
a Gun, Cartouch-Box,
Sword, the Caſe-Bottle, a
ſmall Box of Sugar, and the
China Bowl ; while we were
landing on the Sand, view-
ing the Rack of our unfor-
tunate Boat, we ſpied at Sea
a large Prow, which yet Ad-
miniſtred but ſmall Comfort
to us, ſeeing no hopes of
Relief from thence; wherefore, like Men that knew
not which Way to direct
our Steps, while we were
turning and looking, ſome-
times one way, and ſome-
times

times another, we at last
espied Three Men, Natives
of the Land, coming toward
us; 'twas in vain to dispute
whether or no we should see
them, for our Boat was ir-
recoverable; wherefore one
taking the Musket, (tho'
hardly able to carry it) a-
nother the Sword, and a
Third making fast the Cartouch Box about his Mid-
dle, we advanced to meet
them; being come within
the space of Ten Yards one
of the other, we stood and
view'd each other; they
plac'd themselves abreast,
the oldest standing in the
Middle, resting their Launces on the Ground; having
stood a small Time, the old
Man cried out, *Datin
Dara Mareo ?* Mr. *Bright*

B 3　　under-

underſtanding the *Malayan* Language, anſwered, *de Pulo Condore*, which Engliſh'd is, whence came you? From *Pulo Condore*; this ſhort Dialogue enſued between them. *Mal. Shoppa Oarim?* What Men are you? *Oarim Engliſe, Engliſhmen.* Mal. *Oppa hadda de proe?* What have you in the Proe? Br. *Empal Merium,* Four Guns. Mal. *Hadda logga Oarim de Pree?* Are there more Men in the Proe? Br. *Teda Hadda oarim Logga de Proe,* there is no more Men in the Proe. *Puggi de manno Muſlecat oarim Buſra?* Where does the Great Man Live? Mal. *Tedda hadda varim buora lomaketta;* there is no Great Man here but my ſelf: Upon which we all bow'd

bow'd our Bodies to him,
and advanced nearer, defiring Mr. *Bright* to ask him
whether he would do us
any Harm, and tell him we
would give him what we
had, which he did. Mal.
Jongon tau cevet, be not fearful, *tedda Oarim Jihate*, we
are no Bad Men. Where-
upon we conducted them to
the Place where our loft
Boat lay, and where we had
left our Things behind us ;
having found them, we
made a Prefent of all we had
brought Afhore to the Old
Man, and after a fhort Difcourfe, walked with him
along the Shore to the
Southward ; after about half
an Hour's Journey the Old
Man went into the Woods,
leaving the Two Young
B 4   ones

ones with us, and bidding
us *Jong on fikett fiket*, (i. e.)
walk on a little ; and in leis
than half an Hour returned
to us with Seven Women
and Girls which he had left
behind him in the Woods
when he came to fpeak with
us. With this Reinforce-
ment we jogg'd on about
a Mile and a half further;
which brought us to the
Mouth of a River, whofe
Bar is not above Eight or
Nine Fathom at high Wa-
ter. The Main of this
River is called *Indowe*, where
we faw the Old Man's Proe,
and a Fire by the Wood's
Side. The Old Man bid us
Dueduet defeena, (i. e.) fit
down, and immediately fent
one of the Young Men to
his Proe, who foon returned

ed with a Basket of Boil'd
Yams, which he gave us,
with some fresh Water and
Salt, bidding us *Moekone*,
(*i. e.*) Eat, which we all
did very heartily, and very
thankfully, the Women sitting about Two Yards from
us.   While we were sitting
here, the Old Man told us
he was Captain *Dequallo*, or
Head of the Sea Coast; that
there was not above Fifteen
Men belonging to the Place
where he lived; that this was
the King of *Jehore*'s Land;
and that it was Three Days
Paffage in one of the Proes
to *Jehore*.

That it was almoft a Day's
Sail to the Iflands of *Pulo
Paffang* and *Pulo Aura*; and
that this Place was much In-
fefted with Tigres and Wild
B 5   Hogs.

Hogs. At the beginning of
this Difcourfe the Captain
Dequallo had fent the Women up the River in the
Proe, and we had fcarce done
talking in this Nature, (the
Difcourfe having lafted a-
bout an Hour and a half)
when we efpied Two Proes
coming down the River
with Ten Men in them; they
came (moft of them)
Laughing to us, and fat
down with their Captain;
they were the hardeft fa-
vour'd Fellows I ever faw in
my Life. However, to one
we prefented the Sword, to
another the Musket, and to
the Captain a pair of *Silver*
Buckles, and *John Bremeridge*
gave him his Gold Ring off
from his Finger. In Requi-
tal of which they treated us
with

with boil'd Rice and Salt. In a farther Difcourfe about the Country, and Poffibility of returning whence we came, the Captain *Dequallo* told us there were Two *Englifh* Ships at *Jehore*; and that if we would give him Fifty Dollars he would carry us thither; but that if in the leaft we failed in our Words he would certainly kill us all. We willingly accepted of the Terms, on Condition there were any *Englifh* Ship there; for we trufted that if any Commander knew our Cafe, he would not for fo fmall a Sum as Fifty Dollars fuffer Five *Englifhmen* to fuffer Death, efpecially confidering it would not be above Two or Three Months Work

Work to clear it again.
This being ended, we all
walk'd back to our loft Proe,
where fome of them went
aboard, and dived into her
Bottom, (for by this Time
fhe had made a Grave for
herfelf, and was full of
Water,) but brought no-
thing up except the Child's
Clouts that were before
mentioned; wherenpon we
went back to the River,
where after a fhort Stay we
all Embark'd on the Old
Man's Proes. Notwith-
ftanding we had before
given them the little we
had, they were fo Infatia-
bly Covetous as to fteal
a Bannyan Coat from us,
and fo very kind as to make
us Paddle them up the River
to their Houfes, where being arrived at about Eight
P. M.

P.M. the Captain *Dequallo.* carried us to his House; where after he had given us a Mat to lye on, they brought us some boil'd Rice, Coco-Nu's, Salt and Water, with which we made a hearty Supper; and after we had returned Thanks to Almighty God, fell into Talk with our Landlord, who told us, amongst the rest, that in Three or Four Days he would carry us to *Jehore*; whichNews was so welcome, that we contentedly laid our selves down to Sleep.

After we had been Three Days Ashoar with Capt. *Dequallo*, he order'd us to hawl his Proe out of the Water, in order to fit her for *Jehore*, which we very joyfully did; Two of us went into the Woods with Two of
them,

them, to bring home the young Trees and Rattans which they cut; but my self not being so nimble-footed as the rest, was left behind with my Bundle, where for the Space of an Hour I was lost, but at last found again by One of the *Malaya's*, and conducted home with my Hands and Face so miserably torn by the Rattans; which before they are skinn'd are full of Prickles, that my Comrades hardly knew me: And to add to our Hardships, Capt. *Dequallo* again threatned us with Death if we fail'd of the Payment of the 50 Dollars. During the Time we were thus busied, One of the Grandees came down the River, who it seems was Superior

perior to thé foremention-
ed Capt. *Dequallo*, who after
Examination concerning us,
told him, If he offer'd to carry us away he would take
his Life. When we heard
this we were again wholly
difheartned, and in great
Fear that we fhould never
get clear of one or other.
While we were in this Confternation, and the Two
Malaya's in Difpute what
they fhould do with us, the
Oldeft of Capt. *Dequallo*'s
Wives came to us, and ad-
vifed us to go to the new
Grandee for Paddy, (or Rice
in the Husk,) which accordingly we did, and he gave
us a Bag, containing about
half a Bufhel ; telling us
withal, that when we had
got the Four Guns out of
the

the Boat we fhould go to *Jehore* along with him, which once more gave us a little Hopes.

On the 6th of *February,* it being then the loweftTide, we went to work, and got up One Gun, which we carried above high Water Mark; next Day we got up another, and carried it to the fame Place, but deferr'd getting up the other Two till the Full Moon, which would happen on the 20th of the faid Month. But the Grandee going up the River to his own Houfe before that Time came we were otherwife employed, fometimes in going down to the Water-fide with Capt. *Dequallo* and his Son, to carry the Fifh they catch'd, which were for the moft most Part Shingrays, that they struck with a Prong as they walk'd along the Shoar. Sometimes we went with him to a new Plantation he had begun to clear, where we help'd him to fell the Trees. When we went to this Plantation, which was nearer the Mouth of the River than his House, we always went Arm'd with great Knives and Lances, be-cause of the Tigers where-with this Place abounds, in-somuch that without the Lances, which they use to Admiration, they dare not stir abroad; nor are the Ri-vers less infested with Alli-gators than the Land with Tigers. Capt. *Dequallo* has another Old Plantation on the Banks of a small River,

that

that runs from the North-
ward into the great one,
about half Way from his
House to the River's Mouth ;
thither he One Day ask'd
Two of us to go with him,
where they found a large
Plantation with Three Houses
in it, set upon Trees Four
times higher than these here,
which are at least Three Yards
from the Ground ; their
Reason for Building them so
high is to defend themselves
from the Fury of the Ti-
gers and Elephants ; by
whom, notwithstanding all
their Care, they had 30 of
their small Complement de-
stroyed in a Year's time, the
Remainder in both Places
being not above 40 Men,
Women and Children. When
our Company return'd they
brought

brought with them Yams, Anno
Sugar-Canes, and Paddy. 170$\frac{2}{7}$.
We have not seen any of
the Elephants, only the Prints
of their Feet, and Dung on
the Ground, and Teeth in
Poffeffion of the Natives.

Capt. *Dequallo* told us of
a Sort of Wild People that
live in the Woods, lying very high on Trees; that they
are very Hairy all over, but
on their Heads and Faces
only where they are bald.
That they are of a Middle
Stature, but Speak not any
thing that they can under-
ftand. Here grow Canes
and Rattans in abundance,
and a very heavy and fine
Sort of Red Wood, called
by the Natives *Coger-lacker*.
Here are alfo the fineft Fire-
Flies I ever faw; fome of
them

them we have taken in the
Day-time, of a Noble Co-
lour, being a Spot of Gold,
in a small White Circle, shew-
ing like Gilt Paper, which in
the Night give an extraordinary clear Light. About
the beginning of the Second
Quarter of the Moon, in
February, One of Capt. *Dequallo's* Sons died in his
House ; and just as the Breath
was going out of his Body,
the eldest of Capt. *Dequallo's*
Wives set up a loud Howl-
ing close by the poor Man's
Side ; which Ceremony the
rest of the Females strictly
observ'd, howling when she
did, and stopping when she
did, which caused the Man
to be 17 or 18 Hours dying.
The Old Woman having
ended her Howling, sent
for

Anno
170$\frac{4}{5}$.

for a Second, who fell to
making a long Prayer to
Mahomet, and that ended, the
First went to Howling a-
gain till he died. The Man
was strangely infected with
the Leprosie, or as nauseous
an Itch; and indeed very
few of them are free of it.
Here are Flies they call Ele-
lephant-Flies, in Colour and
Shape much like our *English*
Flies, but bigger. These no
sooner touch you but they
fetch Blood. Another Sort
there are call'd August;
which tho' less than a Mus-
keto, yet raise a Blister as
big as a Horse Bean. There
were none of us but suf-
fer'd by these Flies. Here
are likewise great Black Ants,
which as soon as they touch
a Man inflict so great a Pain,
that

Anno 170¾.

that you would think you were losing a Limb. These Ants never trouble any Body before Sun-rise, and after Sun-set, and are generally found in Dirt and Nastiness.

Soon after came down the River another Grandee, who said he was Captain of the Men in the Woods, and Bought Canes for the Merchants at *Jehore.* He spoke *Portugueze*; and when he knew our Circumstances, seem'd to be in a great Passion because we were not carried to the King of *Jehore*; telling Capt. *Dequallo* that we were not People that used to live on Rice alone; that we eat a great deal of Meat; and that if we were kept here much longer we should die; and told us it

was

was no Matter for his Father-in-law, he would carry us to *Jehore* in his Proe; and withal gave us some Salt-Fish; and told us again, that when he came back out of the small River he would certainly carry us away; and that he was a Greater Man than the Great Man his Father; that he Sold the People Arse-clouts, and took Canes for them. I ask'd how he would Sell Canes? He told me for 3 Dollars *per* Hundred. I have ask'd others the same Question, who would take 2 Dollars or an Arse-clout *per* Hundred.) We began all of us to have a good Opinion of the Captain of the Woods, in hopes he would carry us away; but were soon defeated.

When

-When the Full Moon was
come that we should have
got the o:her Two Guns
aſhoar, but neither of the
Grandees came down to
us, we then began to fear
that this threatning to kill
one another might occaſion
ſome of them to kill us;
but while we were in this
terrible Conſternation, down
came the Captain of the
Woods again, and told us
he would go and prepare his
Proe, and when he came
down again, would certainly
carry us to the King of *Jehore.* Two Days after this
we accompanied the Captain
of the Wood. and Eight of
his Men to the Sea-ſide to
ſee our loſt Boat, where one
of his Men taking our Lin-
guiſter, Mr. *Bright,* aſide,
                    deſired

defired him to give our Gold
to his Mafter, becaufe he
was a greater Man than his
Father, his Anfwer was, that
he had none, (if we had a-
ny to be fure we fhould have
taken Care enough to have
kept it from them.)

Being come back again to
our Home, the Captain *Dequallo*'s Houfe, we the next
Morning difcours'd the Captain of the Woods, to found
whether he ftill continued
in the Mind of carrying us
to *Jehore* ; but found that
after his Knowledge of our
Wants his Defign of fur-
thering our Voyage (or rather his own Interefts) Va-
nifhed, by his telling us he
defign'd to ask Liberty of
of the Great Man his Father-
in-Law, than whom he had

C   before

before told us he was greater. About the latter End
of the Month of *February* a
fmall Junk come from *Cambodia*, and bound to the
Ifland *Timoan*, was by ftrefs
of Weather drove afhore
near our Boat, but after
getting off again, tho' in
no Condition to go to Sea,
they let her drive into the
River, on the North-fide
of the Mouth of which
they Built themfelves Houfes, got afhore the greateft
part of their Goods, and
fell to Building on Two
Boats belonging to their
Wreckt Junk ; there were 14
of them, proportionate clean-
limb'd Men ; they never
ventur'd up the River, but
ftood on their Guards where
they were, which put worfe
Thoughts

Thoughts into us of those we were with than we had before entertain'd, seeing People of the same Faith, speaking the same Language, and living after the same Manner, would have no Commerce with them, but with Sword in Hand; upon which we were resolved, (if our Natives of *Indowe* did not, before the departure of these *Cambodia* Men, prove as good as their Words,) to apply our selves to them for a Passage from thence with them. About this time likewise came into this River from *Pulo Clura* a great Proe laden with Cocoa-Nuts, Seery, and Beetle-Nuts, to truck for Paddy. I shall forbear giving an Account of these

C 2 Fruits,

Fruits, it being fo often and truly done by others. To the Nockidy of this Proe we gave a Note written with Lead, and fubfcribed by us all, telling him our whole Story, and defiring him to give it the firft *Eng-lifh* Ship he fhould light upon, which he promifed to do, but could by no means be perfwaded to take any of us with him from this our now loathfom Habitation.

Soon after this there came in here another Proe from *Pulo Timoan* laden as the laft, but they would not fuffer any of us to go aboard, whether out of Fear of us, or of the Government they were under, I can't tell. *Sunday* the 14th of *March* came
down

down the River the Gran-
dee who had before fet us to
Work to Weigh the Guns,
and by whofe Order we
have ever fince had our
Paddy, who told us fo foon
as he had got up the other
Two Guns he would carry
us with him to *Jehore*.
This Evening the Captain
of the Woods came like-
wife down with his Proe.
On *Monday* the 15th in the
Morning we went down the
River to get up the other
Two Guns, but came fo
late that the Tide of Flood
was fet in, and the Water
rifen fo much, that we could
do no more but fling One
Gun before we were forc't
to leave off Work. On the
16th we all , except the
Captain of the Woods, re-

C 3   turn'd

turn'd to our Works of get-
ing up the Two Guns, and
foon got up that which we
had before flung; but while
we were doing it down
came the Captain of the
Woods in his Proe, but
made no flop, going directly
over the Bar (as the Men
told us) for *Jehore*, which
Action put us again into a
Fright; for when we faw
him, gone who had fo often
promifed to carry us with
him we were afraid the o-
ther would have ferved us
the fame Sauce when he
had got what he could by
us, and fo at laft we fhould
be left to ftarve; the fore-
mentioned Grandee, whom
we now underftood to be
his Father-in-Law, feem'd
very much difturb'd at the
Action,

Action, the rest of the Men telling us the Captain of the Woods was *Bohun, & Oarim Johatt*, (i. e.) Not good, and a Rogue-Man. That he was gone to *Jehore* to acquaint the King with what had pass'd, in expectation of getting that to himself which belonged to his Father in-Law; but being somewhat come to himself, he bid us make haste and get the other Gun up, that we might be going too. We very joyfully went about it, and soon accomplish'd it, laying them Two with the other Two. And here I must take Notice, that tho' at low Water 3 Yards beyond the Boat it was not deeper than a Man's Middle, yet in

C 4　the

the Boat there was Nine
Foot Water, fo deep a
Grave fhe had made for herfelf. Being return'd to the
Town we liv'd in, we had
Orders to beat our Paddy,
and get in readinefs to Embark that Night, which we
very joyfully did, being
gladded with the Thoughts
of once more feeing *Europeans*, by whofe Affiftance we
might again fee our Friends
and Relations, which we before almoft defpair'd of.

March the 17th, about 4
this Morning, we took our
Departure from the *Malayan*
Town, and our Leaves of
our Heathen Friends, Row-
ing down the River in a
fmall Proe, where were Ten
of us, *viz.* the Grandee, and
4 of his Men, befides us five:
Being

Being come down to the Anno
Rivers Mouth we went a-- 170$\frac{2}{7}$.
fhore to take in frefh Water,
which when we had done
we Rowed out of the River,
and about 8 got clear of the
Iflands which we had fo
Fruitlefly attempted in our
own Boat ; but now hav-
ing gentle Gales, clear Weather, and fmooth Water,
we kept along Shore, the
Boat going clearly through,
and having the Advantage
of a Light Moon, we kept
on our Way all Night. The
18th having moderate Gales
and fair Weather, we all
this Day kept the Shore a-
bout Two Miles diftant, till
about 4 *P. M.* when we
handed our Sail, and betook
our felves to Rowing to-
ward the Land, at 5 Ancho-

red within 100 Yards of the
Sand, there being but little
Surf; the Land is low, and
shows itself full of broken
Ground and small Rocks,
whereof some under Water.
The Anchor not holding, we
drove upon a Rock , where
we struck twice, but took no
harm, whereupon we gathered in the Cable till it was almost up and down, and then
took a Hitch with it about a
Staff, which we stuck well in
the Ground, and then veer'd
away again; thus we rid all
Night. Here is a small River
which runs parallel to the
Sea-shore at a small distance
from it. On the Land between
both Two of the *Malayans*
went ashore with their Lances in their Hands to look for
Turtle Eggs, but found none.
                          While

While they wꞏre aſhore their
Captain told us the People
who lived there were not
good, that they blew poiſon'd
Darts and threwSumpets. I ob-
ſerv'd thoſe that went aſhore
kept together , and did not
venture out of our Sights.

On the 19th at 5 *A. M.*
being got under Sail with
fair Weather and a fine
Gale, the Captain told us that
perhaps we might ſee Proes,
deſiring us if we did to lye
down cloſe, and be very ſi-
lent , for that if it were
known there were any *Engliſhmen* in the Proe, not only we, but they too, ſhould
be killed for the Sake of
Gold, without a great deal
of which they ſuppoſe *Engliſhmen* never go ; we ſaw
indeed 3 Proes, but too far
off

off to make any Surprize, had
they been so minded. A-
bout 4 *P. M.* we got to the
Mouth of the River *Jehore*,
where were several Boats,
which inform'd us there was
never a Ship at *Jehore*, but
that there were Two *Dutchmen* living in the Town, of
which we were not a little
glad.

It was some Consolation
to us to hear that we should
now again Converse with
Christians, tho' in the midst
and Power of *Mahometans.*
While we were Rowing up
the River we were Five or
Six Times hail'd from the
Shore, on which Occasions
I could not but return
Thanks to God, for that he
had favour'd us with so dark
a Night that we could not
be

be publickly feen; being obliged to paddle our Heathen
Friends (or rather Mafters)
up the River. Being at a-
bout 9 *P. M.* arrived at *New
Jehore,* we found Six great
China Junks, and feveral
Proes, moared abreaft the
Town, where we came to
an Anchor, Sleeping all Night
in the Proe.

On the 20th in the Morn-
ing about 8 the Captain,
who came with us from *Indowe,* carried us before one of
the Chans or Captains here
at *Jehore,* who Conducted us
all to the Generals, to whom
the *Indowe* Captain told all
our Adventures as we had
related them to him, from
thence we were Conducted
before the King, who im-
mediately fent for one of the
Dutch-

Dutchmen to be his Linguifter, telling us he had fent
for one of our Country-men,
which made fome of us be-
lieve when we faw him
coming that he had been
an *Englishman.* When he
had performed his Ceremo-
nies to the King, he fat down
at his Left Hand next but
Two to him, while we Five
fat on the Ground facing
them.

The King talk'd near half
an Hour with this *Hollander*,
who fpeaking a little broken *English*, at laft faid, *Well,
Brothers, the King bids me
ask whether you will live on this
Land* ; we defired him to
tell him *No :* That we were
Servants to the *English* Company fettled at the Ifland
Pulo Condore, from whence
we

we had been drove after the
manner already related to
him, and that we only begg'd
the Favour to let us pass for
Malacca; which he positive-
ly deny'd; then some of
his Nobles were at us to
Slarn, (*i. e.*) be Circumcised,
and be of their Belief, telling us what great Matters
we might expect, as Wives,
Money, &c. but we all re-
fused it, begging that we
might pass to *Malacca*; but
were again deny'd, and told,
that when any Ship came
here bound for *Pulo Con-
dore* we might if we wou'd go
away in her: Our Answer
was, that the Ships that came
there did for the most part
belong to the Country; that
'twas very rare for any
Ships bound to *Pulo Con-
dore*

dore or *China* to come there,
except through their late-
nefs in thofe Seas, they were
nipt by the Eafterly *Monfoons*,
fo as they could not reach
the Coaft ; and therefore we
once more humbly begg'd
for Liberty to go to *Malacca*, but were again deny'd,
and withal difmifs'd from
the King's Prefence , and
conducted back to the Generals, or *Datto Bandaro*, who
again told us we muft Slarn's
but we all agreed rather to
die, and told him we would
never do it ; that we would
rather fuffer all they could
impofe on us than deny our
Lord and Saviour Jefus
Chrift. Whereupon after
a fhort Difcourfe among
themfelves they gave us a
Bag of Rice, and *Datto Bandaro*

daro gave us a Gold Dollar to buy Fish withal to eat
with our Rice, for which
we all bow'd to him in To-
ken of Gratitude, and then
were conveyed to a House
into which they put Caft-away Men, and thofe defigned to be the King's Slaves.
The Name they have for
this Place is *Poonurlue* and
Baililee it is a fquare Place
or Compound, containing
9 or 10 Houfes ; here it is
that the Chan or Captain
lives to whom we were firft
brought ; he has the Charge
of all Prifoners committed
to him, which are for the
moft part either Caft-away
Men, or thofe taken by War
or Surprize, and belong to
the King, except taken on
the Sea or Land bordering
on

on *Datto Bandaro's*, for then
he takes his firſt Choice. We
have been told by the Inhabitants of *Jehore* that this
Datto Bandaro has as much
Land as the King; that this
preſent King had Murther-
ed the other with his own
Hands; that he who is *Datto
Bandaro* at the Death of
the King ſucceeds in the
Throne, this having been
the Title of the preſent King
in the Reign of the former,
who had been Murthered
about Six Years ago, he being a very Tyrannical Prince,
who never miſs'd a Day
without killing one or o-
ther with his own Hands
on very frivolous Occaſions.
But to return to our ſelves,
tho' we had a Priſon for
our Habitation, it was not
made

made fo to us, we being allowed the Liberty of the
Town Proes, *China* Junks,
or where elfe we pleas'd ;
they knew the fmall Hopes a
Stranger could have of get-
ing away, except he could
propofe to live in the
Woods among Wild Beafis,
as Tigers, Wild Hogs,
Musk-Cats and Elephants,
wherewith they abound.
There are feveral *China*-
Men which Live and Trade
in this Place. Here we faw
a Man who is reported to
have been maintain'd in
Splendor by the late King
of *Jehore Raja Coohefle*, his only Bufinefs being to Murther
thofe to whom his Mafter
was not well Affected.

But the prefent King *Raja
Bufra* being a more Merciful

ful Man, and of a Milder
Temper, having no Occasi-
on for this Inhuman Butcher,
who is now called *Conechine*,
or Cat, fuffers him to beg
Alms about the Street; he
is a very Miferable Wretch
to look at, and is (or out
of Policy feigns to be) turned to a very Natural.

We had now been Four
Days without hearing from
either the King or *Datto Bandaro*, when on the 24th the
Dutch Renegado came to us
to Conduct us to *Datto Bandaro's*; we were in Hopes it
had been about our going to
Malacca, but when we came
there found the quite contrary, for we found him
with a Convocation of Cler-
gy-men, who as foon as
we were come, again put it

to

to us to Slarn, telling us
if we did they would give
us Wives and Gold in a-
bundance ; and that if we
did not like staying with
them we might afterwards
go where we pleased, but
if we refused they threatned
us with Death, which we all
told them we would chuse
as the least of the Two E-
vils. Upon which one of
chiefest of them came and
sat himself close by me, and
put the same Question to
me, which I answer'd with
a hasty No: With that he
put the side of his Hand to
my Neck drawing, it twice
back and forward, thereby
signifying he would cut off
my Head, upon which I likewise put my Hand to my
Neck, crying, *Masche*, a
Word

Word in common ufe imply-
ing what fignifies it ? And
in haftily taking away my
Hand again chanc'd to ftrike
him on the Neck ; upon
that, without fpeaking a
Word more to me, he rifes
up and tells the General,
that the long Man was very
crofs, and that he was General of the reft, (as I was
inform'd by them who un-
derftood him better than
my felf ;) foon after this we
were difmifs'd for that time,
having a fmall Bag of Rice
given us by Order of *Datto
Bandaro* ; in the Afternoon
the *Dutch* Renegado came
to us, (as he faid,) by *Datto
Bandaro*'s Order to conduct
us to the King. Now I
expected fome of us fhou'd
have been put to Death, according

cording to the Promises and
Threats of their Priests, but
encouraged my self with
Hopes of a Pardon for all
my Sins, through the Mer-
cy and for the Sake of Jesus
Christ my Saviour and Re-
deemer, for whose Name **I**
was about to die, perswa-
ding my self, that if I now
denied the Faith I had been
so often confirmed in, I
should be infallibly doom-
ed to Eternal Damnati-
on.

We endeavoured to con-
firm one another in unmove-
able Resolutions to see un-
dauntedly Death's Fright-
ful Face for the Sake of the
Christian Religion. The
Dutchman began with dismal
reiterated Protestations to
assure us, that if we now
refused

refufed the King to Slarn
we muft never expect to go
hence alive, holding up his
Hands, and calling the Sun
to Witnefs the Truth of his
Words ; telling us he had
been forc'd to do the fame
himfelf, notwithftanding
which he faid he was a good
Chriftian in his Heart. That
it was out of his Love to
Chrift, and the Chriftian
Faith, that he told us what
he did ; and that they never
forc'd him to go to their
Churches ; and then pulling
out a Common-Prayer-Book
he fell to Reading, withal
telling us, *No, Brothers, you
are mightily miftaken in me,
my Heart is the fame toward
God now as ever it was, al-
though I was forc'd (to fave
my Life) to do what I have
done*

done; and then told us a Anno
Story, that being one time 170⅔.
discovered by them as he
was Reading in his Prayer-
Book, and Praying to God,
they ask'd him what Book it
was? He told them a Book
for Gunners and Pilots; with
which Answer being satisfied,
they had never more ask'd
him any Question about it,
tho' they often saw him make
use on't. Having ended his
Story, we told him, if the
Case were so that we must
either die, or yield to their
wicked Impositions, we had
all resolved upon Death.

Being now arrived at the
King's Palace, they all went
into his Presence, except my
self, who staid behind at the
Corner of the State-House,
to offer up my Prayers to

D   Almighty

Almighty God for Pardon
of my Sins, and to ſtrength-
en me in the Faith of his
Son Jeſus Chriſt our Saviour, ſo as not to fall from
it for any Pangs of Death ;
but had not been long there
ee'r I was ſent for by the
King's Order, and accord-
ingly went in and ſate down
on the Ground by my other
Conſorts. They told us if
we did not aſſent ro their
Propoſitions we muſt ex-
pect nothing but Death ; for
the more ready Execution
of which they had placed
Men by us with Naked Cree-
ſes in their Hands, who we
expected (upon our Refu-
ſals) were to have obeyed
their Bloody Commands.

It being demanded of me
what Anſwer I would give ?
I

I. defired Mr. *Bright* to tell
the King, that fhould I confent to any fuch thing, the
King of *England* would
me put to Death there;
and that it was better to die
here than before my Friends
and Relations; that there
were feveral *China* Men here
who knew me when I be-
long'd to the King's Ship
which was loft in *China*, that
could averr the Truth of
what I faid. To which the
King returned Anfwer, That
I was then on his Territories;
faying Angrily, that God
had given us all to him, and
bid us chufe whether we
would Slarn or Die? I told
them I would chufe Death;
after which they lookt very
grimly on me, but faid no
more to me, I being affign'd
D 2   for

for Death ; but the other
Four were by the dreadful
Looks of Death affrighted
from that which before they
thought they could have
ftood to, tho' aſſaulted by
Death in all its moſt diſmal
Appearances. While I waited for my Doom, the King
fell to talking with his Nobles, which he continued for
near half a quarter of an
Hour, and then gave 3 Gold
Dollars to the other Four,
but ordered them to give
me nothing of it, nor ſuffer
me to Eat any thing bought
with it, and then diſmiſs'd
us, *Oarim Pangong*, (*i. e.*)
Longman, (by which Name
they diſtinguiſhed me) being
ordered to be ſtarved ; but
ſome of our People thought
(I believe) their Food would
do

do them no good if I went Anno
without; whereupon it was 170?.
agreed, not without jang-
ling, that I fhould partake
with them. Mr. *Bright* gave
me his Coat, Hat, and a
Blue Shirt, and *Edward Bethall* gave me another Shirt;
other Cloaths being defigned for them. I told them
it might be now in their
Power to prevent what I
Hourly expected, and fave
my Life ; they all promifed
their Endeavours on my behalf, for now I was forc'd
to be obliging, knowing how
much it concerned my Safety
to be in their Favour at this
time, when I expected Day
and Night to be killed by
fome of the Natives ; for it
was but a Word of the
King's, or *DattoBandaro*'s, and

Anno
170¾. it might be done, without
ever being ask'd why it
was, either by Day or
Night.

Anno
1703. *March* 26. the *Dutch*
Renegado came to tell us
that *Datto Bandaro* wanted to
fpeak with all Five of us next
Morning, at which time we
promifed to wait on him;
and the next Day, according
to Order, we all went to
wait on *Datto Bandaro*; but
he having private Bufinefs,
were deferr'd till the Mor-
row. Next Morning we be-
ing defigned not to go near
any of them till fent for a-
gain, one of us told the
reft, that if they would not
he would go to get fome
Arfe-Clouts, but was difwa-
ded by the reft, they praying
to God that fome Accident
might

might happen to avert that
Wickednefs they were (for
fear of Death) running into. *John Bremeridge* told
me, that notwithftanding
what he had faid then, he
would now die with me,
feeming to be very forrow-
ful; I told him I wifht to the
Lord they had all ftood to
their Words then; that it was
my Belief they would not
have put us all to Death,
for fear the Chriftians fhould
at one time or other revenge
our Death. The 29th *Na-
thaniel Packet* was as good as
his Word, (tho' much Per-
fwafion was ufed to hinder
him from going,) and went
to *Datto Bandaro*, who fent
him back again to fetch the
reft of us; being come before
him he gave each of us a

D 4.   Piece

Piece of White Cloth about
3 Yards and a Halflong, and
Ell wide, but I refufed it
upon any Account of yeild-
ing to be cut ; but Mr. *Bright*
told me that *Datto Bandaro*
faid I might do what I would
with it; upon which I received it at Mr. *Bright's* Hands,
Here was in Company *Datto
Bandaro*, the Captain of the
Woods, and the Great Capt.
who brought us in his Proe to
Jehore. I believe during our
Paffage he had heard fome of
us fing, and told *Datto Bandaro* of it, by his asking us to
fing One or Two of our *Englifh* Songs, which we moft of
us did, and pleafed him fo
well that he gave us an *Englifh* Quart Bottle full of Rack,
and fome Cocoa-nuts ; and
then rifing up, he went out
of

of this Houfe, which is the
Place where he receives Vi-
fits, and difpatches Bufinefs
of State, and bid us follow
him. From thence he car-
ried us to his private Houfe,
where he keeps his Women,
and defired us to fing before
them. After finging a-
bout haif a Dozen Songs
we were difmifs'd without a
Word of the Old Tale.

In the Morning *Datto
Bandaro* fent for us again ;
Four of us went to him, and
when we came found the
Bufinefs was to go in a Proe
with him, to fhoot at a Mark,
and accordingly a fmall Brafs
Gun with Powder and Shot
was brought us, and by
Three of us carried down to
the River fide ; when we
had placed it in its Carriage,
and put it on Board a large

Anno
1703.

D 5   Proe,

Proe, Mr. *Bright*, *Bethall*,
and my felf, Imbark'd with
Datto Bandaro, and feveral
other Grandees, on Board the
fame Proe. After we had
paddled them pretty well o-
ver the River, we were ordered to load the Gun,
which we did, then having
fet up a fmall Redjan on
the Bank of the River, they
paddled about half a Mile
from it, and ordered us to
Fire, which we all did in
our Turns, my laft Shot
ranging clofe by the Lar-
board-fide of the Mark was
by all their Approbations
much the beft ; from thence
they carried us to the South-
moft Fort, ftanding on the
fame fide of the River with
the Town ; it is built upon
a fmall rifing on a Point,
made by a fmall River running

ning into the great One.
It is mounted with Twelve
Brass Guns, seeming very fair
to the Eye, Five of which
command cross the great River, and the other Seven
down it, guarding the En-
trance of the small One. We
were ordered to Fire one of
those looking over the River,
carrying a 9 *l.* Shot; after
we had laden it, and brought
it (by all our Judgments) to
bear on the Mark allotted,
Datto Bandaro having taken
his Sight, bid us if we
thought we ewere well to Fire
it, which *Edward Bethall*
did, and had assuredly hit
the Mark, had not the Carriage been so much too low
for the Port that the Gun
could not be laid under Met-
tle. This Fort is a long
Square, built with thick
Logs

Logs of Wood, laid one on the other 12 Foot from the Ground on the outside, and has a Level raifed within about Five Foot; the Ports are all cut fo fmall that a Man can't traverfe a Gun Four Points both Ways. During our ftay here the *Malayan* Gunner was very eager and hot in perfwading me to turn, telling me how Rich a Man I fhould foon be, and was back'd both by *Datto Banduro* and the reft of the Grandees; but I defired Mr. *Bright* to give the fame Anfwer I had before given the King; they bid Mr. *Bright* tell me they would bind me Hand and Foot, and Cut or Circumcife me by Force.

I told them they might indeed Cut and Kill me too, but
                            while

while my Resolutions re-
main'd firm and unshaken
it would avail nothing ; having ended such like Dif-
courses, we all returned to
the Town, and after we had
waited on the General to
his House, retired to our
Lodging, the *Bailile* ; in the
Evening of the same Day
he sent for us again by one
of his Servants, who after
Supper conducted us to his
private House, where he and
his Women were. At our
first coming he treated us
with Beetle-Nut, Seery, Pine-
Apples, and Sugar-Canes,
and then desired us to sing
and dance after the *English*
Fashion, all which we did:
For my part I show'd him the
trick of cutting a String in
Two, knotting it again,
and then sliding the Knot so
un-

unperceivably away while
he held both Ends in his
Hands, that it might feem to
be made whole again, he
was fo well pleafed with the
Whim, that he would needs
fee it done again, laughing
all the time very heartily.
After a little more finging
and dancing he difmiffed us,
and fent one of his Servants
to guard us home.

The 31ft we were again
fent for by *Datto Bandaro*;
Mr. *Bright* and *Bethall* went
to know his Commands, to
each of whom he gave a
Clout to wrap about their
Middles, and a Gettarry for
their Heads; he gave Mr.
Bright a Paper with fomething Written in it to be got-
ten by Heart, and fent home
Two Guns by them to be
clean'd.

clean'd. I would not fo much as look on the Paper, as believing it to contain little good, and told them, they that took the Guns might for my Part clean them. Mr. *Bright* told me there was an Ambaffador come from the King of *Camboidia*, that he was afraid I, or whoever fhould Recant what they had faid, would be fent to him as Slaves; and that *Datto Bandaro* had told him of my cutting the String in Two, and making it whole again : This Evening the King fent for us ; Four went, leaving *Nath. Packet* to prepare Supper; being come into his Prefence he defired us to fing and dance, which we did, and *John Bremeridge* and *Edward Bethall* tumbled, and walkt

on

on their Hands; the Women
came not into the Room, but
crowded at the Doors and
Windows to fee us play the
Mountebanks for their Di-
verfion ; and I (to hold up
my Credit with them) fhow'd
them a Trick, which was to
make two Stones Dance, at
which they all laughed very
heartily. The King again
put the Old Queftion to me
by Mr. *Bright*, and received
the Old Anfwer ; notwith-
ftanding which he fnow'd no
Signs of Anger in his Face,
as at other times he had done ;
his Looks were mightily altered, and his Countenance
difcovered he was well-plea-
fed. Having detained us
till near 12 at Night, he at
laft difmiffed us with a Gold
Dollar, and put Mr. *Bright*
and

and *Bethall* in *Malayan* Habits.

April the 1st we were sent for by the King to reiterate last Night's Merriment; after which he demanded of me to Slarn, but received the same Answer; upon which Mr. *Bright* told the King's Brother, that if the King would suffer the other Four to go to *Malacca* he would on that Account be Circumcised; who proposed it to the King, but was bid to hold his Tongue, for he would keep us all, and then dismiss'd us for that time. The 4th Mr. *Bright* and *Nathaniel Packet* went to *Datto Bandaro's*, who gave them a Bag of Rice, and *Packet* a Cloth to put about his Middle, and enquired whether any of us had

had got that Writing in the Paper by Heart? But was told we had not. This Day some of the *China* Men coming to pay us a Visit, they were so disgusted at the Sight of Mr. *Bright* and the other in *Malayan* Habits, that they went away without speaking, tho' they had before spoke very kindly to us, and sometimes given us Money, tho' not much. The 6th Four of us went to *Datto Bandaro*, but he not being at his Publick House, Mr. *Bright* went to his Private House to him, where being admitted, he told him in the Name of us all that we desired some Money to buy Fish. He gave him a Gold Dollar, and enquir'd after the rest of us; Mr. *Bright* told him Two of us were

were Sick, whereupon he asked whether or no Women
would make us well, and
bid him whenever he wanted
any thing not to be fearful
of coming to his Houfe, he
and we being now all one.

The 9th our Rice being
fpent, *Nat. Packet* went to
Datto Bandaro for more ,
and had a Bag given him,
which he brought home :
This Morning fome of the
Malaya's ftole 600 Petty's out
of the Houfe; they belonged
to my felf and *John Bremeridge*, and was our fhare of the
laft Dollar given us by *Datto
Bandaro*; for *John Bremeridge* and I eat by our felves,
and the other Three by themfelves, and had done fo during the greateft Part of our
ftay at *Indowe*.

Next

Next Morning a *China* Man,
known by the Name of *Ber-
go*, with whom I had formerly been well acquainted at
Amoy, and who now belonged to a Junk at this Place,
came to fee me, to whom I
related *Jack*'s Lofs and mine ;
and having enquired into the
Sum he gave us every Petty,
and promifed to give me in a
Day or Two fome Paper,
China Ink, and Goofe-quills,
for which I had asked him ;
and that he would acquaint
the Commanders of all the
Ships he met with how we
were detain'd here, and how
we were ufed. Next Day
Nat. Packet went to *Datto
Bandaro* for more Rice, which
was given him ; and being
ask'd after the reft of us, he
faid we were Sick. *Edward
Bethall*

Bethall going that Afternoon on Board the Junk to which *Beago* belonged, I defired he would put him in Mind of the Paper, Ink, and Quills he had promifed me. The Paper and Ink he gave him, but faid he could not get a-ny *Hair of de Goofe* ; *Bethall* could not dive into his mean-ing, but could get no other Name from *Beago*, who told him, *You Fool-Man, you know Savy de Hair of de Goufe? Go tell Mr.* Vaughan *he Savy for de Hair of de Goofe.* The 15th was a Feftival Day with the Natives, both the Poor and Rich putting on their Fineft Apparel. A-bout Noon the King fate in the Publick Houfe on the Right Hand as you go into the Palace , the Pillars of which

which were covered with
Cotten Cloth of all Colours,
and the Roof hung with as
great variety of very Rich
Silks.   At the upper End of
the Hall the King was seated
in a small raised Square, hung
round with very Fine Silk
Curtains decently furled, so
as that he might be seen.

The House was round be-
set with a great Number of
Wax Candles, and for a farther Augmentation of the
Solemnity, all his Musick was
plac'd in another House not
far distant, where they con-
tinually play'd during the
time the King sate thus ex-
pofed to Publick View, *Datto Bandaro*, with all the King's
Women and his own, were
at their Devotions in the *Pagoda*, that is, to the Eastward
of

of *DattoBandaro*'scompound.
Having ended their Devo-
tions, they all (both Cler-
gy and Laity) made a Solemn
and Regular Proceffion with
Mufick before them to the
Palace, where being arriv'd,
all was ended with the Noife
of Mufick and Firing of
Guns, but with fo great a Si-
lence of the Natives, as was
admirable, and quite contrary to the Practice of *Europeans* on fuch Occafions, every
one feeming to be afraid left
he fhould be heard by the
next to him.

They continued their So-
lemnities the next Day, (or
rather finifhed them) by
bringing the neweft and
largeft of their *Pago-
da*'s Two large Buffoloes,
which they ftak'd down
by

Anno by the Four Legs on the Eaſt
1703. Side of the *Pagoda*.   After
their Prieſts had ended their
Devotions, the Supream of
them cut both their Throats,
and then went away, leaving
them Dead on the Spot, till
next Morning. Mr. *Bright*
was at *Datto Bandaro*'s, where
he ſaw above Sixty Fowls
with their Throats likewiſe
cut by one of their Prieſts.
About 7 in the Morning all
the *China* Men in the Place,
to the Number of about 600
Perſons, Arm'd with Scime-
ters, Small-Arms, or Swords
and Targets, march'd with
China Plays ; but (whether
by the King's Order or not
I can't tell) they ſoon broke
off from that, and fell to
ſhewing the King their Way
of Fighting with their long
Scime-

Scymitars, and their Method
of shifting their Targets,
which some of them did very dextrously. This Day also was ended with Musick,
and firing of Guns. The
17th the Captain of the *Bailile* made a Feast in our
Room, it being hung over
Head with painted Linen
Cloth, and the Floor laid
with the finest Sort of Matts.
The Guests were all in their
Richest Habits, and the
Treat consisted of Beetle-
Nut, Seery, Fowls, Rice, and
Fruit. At Night he sent us a
Dish of Pilloe, and part of a
Fowl. This Day Mr. *Bright*
went to wait on the King,
and *Packet* on *Datto Banda-
ro* ; *Packet* brought home a
Bag of Rice, and Mr. *Bright*
a *Copang*. The Captains of
E the

the *China* Junks having perfwaded us to go to *Datto
Bandaro* to procure our Freedom, promifing if we could
get the Government's Liberty they would carry us with
them, and give us Money.
We went to him and begg'd
very heartily to let us go,
or if not all, that at leaft he
would fuffer one to go,
which put him into fuch a
fret, that he not only refufed us, but when we ask'd
for Money, would neither
give us that, nor an Anfwer,
tho' we waited near Two
Hours for one. When we
came Home again we found
one of the Natives made a
Prifoner in our own Room,
having his Legs faft in a
Wooden pair of Stocks; this
Man had formerly been Ma-
fter

ster of one of their biggest
Proes; his Crime it seems
was, that when *Datto Banda-*
ro sent for him, he sent
Word he would not go,
and withal reflected on the
Government, which being
reported to *Datto Bandaro*
he sent for him by force, and
heard the same Words from
his own Mouth, upon which
he committed him to Prison.
The 21st Mr. *Bright* and
Packet went to wait on
Datto Bandaro ; *Packet*
brought Home a Bag of
Rice, but Mr. *Bright* could
not get any Money; so
much the Disgust lately taken
reigned still. Upon which I
set up for a Doctor, (Necessity
being the Mother of Inventi-
on) in which Employ proving
successful, I got many Pa-

tients

tients, and a little Money wherewith to supply my Necessities. *Bright* and *Packet* went again next Day to *Datto Bandaro*, whom they now found in a better Humour, and brought Home a Gold Dollar, which we shared among us. In the Morning *Datto Bandaro* sent for us all Five, and when we were come before him, desired us to Sing, Dance, and shew some Pastime, which we comply'd with, and after Three Hours stay, and a Treat of Pine-Apples, Sugar-Canes and Beetle-Nuts, &c. were dismiss'd. The 26th I met with a great Moor Merchant, lately come from *Syam*, who would needs have me go to his House with him, but would not suffer

me

me to call any of the reft, Anno
tho' we went clofe by the 1703.
Bailile. Being come Home
he treated me with Pilloe,
dry'd Roes of Fifh extraordinary well dreft, and feveral Sorts of Fruit; after
which he fent for another
Moor Man, who fpake *Por-*
tuguezze, to be Interpreter between us; when he was come
he fhow'd me a Veffel he defigned to Buy, and told me
he would procure the King's
Leave, and carry me with him
to *Bengall* ; but if he failed of that, I fhould take no
Notice of it to any Body,
and he would convey me a-
way without his Knowledge,
at which I was not a little
glad. About the beginning
of *May* our Four Guns arrived from *Indowe* ; *Datto Ban-*

E 3　　　　　*daro*

Anno
1703.

daro going down to the River Side to view them, fent for us to affift in getting them out, which we did: From thence he fent them to the *Buzzar*, or *Market-Place*, at the lower End of which they were plac'd. Soon after there came to Anchor, abreaft the Town a *Portugueze* Sloop and a *Moors* Ship from *Cudda*; the Sloop had Two *European Portugueze* belonging to her, whereof the Captain was one, but aboard the Ship was never a Chriftian. The *Portugueze* Captain told Mr. *Bright* he wou'd endeavour to procure our Liberty; that on that Account he would make a Prefent to *Datto Bandaro*, which with us he would carry before him; that if he accepted his
Pre-

Present he would deliver
that with one Hand, and
take us away with the other.
Ten Days after her Arrival
the Ship sail'd for *Camboidia*,
carrying with her one of the
Renegado *Dutchmen.* A Fire
happened near the River's
Side, which occasioned a con-
fused Noise thro' the whole
Town, every one taking the
Cry from another, and running Distractedly about,
tho' I believe few knew why
they did so. After the Fire
was put out, which was in
less than an Hour, one of
the Grandees ask'd me what
Method we used when a Fire
hapned in *England?* I told
him we made use of Engines
that would throw Water very high and far, with much
Violence, and if that fail'd

E 4   by

by reafon of the fierceneſs
of the Fire, and thickneſs of
the Houſes, we blew up that
next to the Houſe on Fire.
After a little Confideration
he told me the only Means
they had was to carry Wa-
ter to it as faſt as they could,
and if that would not do it
muſt take its Courſe. About
the middle of the Month
Mr. *Bright, Bethall* and *Packet* went to live with one
Abdruma, a *Moor man* that
had loft his Caſt, but *John
Bremeridge* and my ſelf remain'd in our Old Lodging. I
was now pretty well Verſed
in my Profeſſion, and got many Patients; and where I had
One might have had Ten,
but did not care to under-
take more than I could well
give Attendance to; the greateſt

eft of the Natives put great Anno
Faith in me, feeing the many 1703.
great Cures I perform'd. I
gave good found Purges and
Sweats, and infallibly Cur'd
Agues after this manner. I
infufed Tamarinds and To-
bacco all Night in Water,
and the next Morning ftrain'd
it, and making it pallata-
ble by Champoring Honey
with it, Adminiftred it at
the time of the Agues coming, (at the fame time giving
them a Charm to hang a-
bout them,) which working
by Vomit, never fail'd of
a perfect Cure in Two or
Three times giving.   Nor
was it Phyfick only I pretended to , for I took the
Skin off a Woman's Right
Eye, which had for fome
Years deprived her of Sight,
to which fhe was by this

Operation petfectly reftor'd;
and to be fhort, I had Salves
for all Sores ; by which
means *John Bremeridge* and
I lived much better than
when we were all Five to-
gether, and enjoyed far greater Content, being now without that Bickering and Noife
which before we were con-
tinually plagu'd with.

I was now mightily in
Favour, enjoying as much
Freedom in the whole Com-
pound as if I had been at
Home with my Relations. A
Great Man that lived in the
Bailile, and his chief Wife,
who was a *Syam* Woman,
would needs have me call
them Father and Mother, as
they did me Child. They
took from us all the Care and
Trouble of dreffing our Vi-
ctuals,

&uals, we conftantly having
our Diet of them, and that as
good as *Datto Bandaro* eat
himfelf.   We had always
Two or Three of their Servants to wait on us ;   from
them we had Cloth to make
Cloaths, and Money whene-
ver we wanted it.   They fur-
nifhed us with Matts and
Pillows to fleep on ;   and if
at any time we ftaid late
with them, might have lain
in their Houfe, which we
fometimes did, but dar'd not
practice it for fear of bringing on them the King's Dif-
pleafure.   This Man had always been Ambaffador to
the Kings of *Atchin* and *Camboidia*, but during the Three
Years laft paft had been
Lame or Dead on the Right
Side, fo as to have loft the
Ufe

Ufe of thofe Limbs, but by
God's Permiffion and my Induftry was fo well recovered,
that with a very little Help
he could Walk, and ufe his
Hand and Arm indifferently
well.   My Father and Mo-
ther (for fo I muft now call
them) would often enquire
of the Age and Number of
my Relations in *England*, as
how many Brothers and Si-
fters I had, and how many
my Father and Mother had,
and how Old they were, all
which I freely told them;
then they would ask me whether I fhould ever think of
them when at home among
my Friends and Relations?
I told them yef, and that I
would never part with fome
Things they had given me;
then my *Syam* Mother would
fay,

say, *Ah anick, anick de Alla-
thoilo sudea cacce leatte dearca-
ponya Ovemai volpa sadarro sadarro porempire catta sia cac-
ca Banyack Tabey,* (i. e.) *Child,
Child, when God Almighty gives
you the Sight of your Father or
Mother, Brothers or Sisters, tell
them that I pay them a very
great Respect.* At other times
they would ask how we prayed to God, and what Posture
we put our selves into on
that Occasion, and when I
told them, would say that
was as they did at *Rome*; but
I told them no, for at *Rome*
they prayed to Images, but
we only prayed to God, and
his Son Jesus Christ; at
which they said they only
prayed to God and *Maho-
met*, but that some *Malaya's*
were so bad as to pray to the
Devil,

Devil, faying, *Billa hollo bike
tedda bulloe Cudgee Johatte
ena, Satan Suda Cudgee Johatte*, (i. e.) God Almighty is
good, and does no Mifchief,
but the Devil does all the
Mifchief. Towards the latter
End of this Month the *China*
Junks prepared to Sail, and
the Prifoner I before fpoke
of was let out of the Stocks,
and had the Liberty of going about the Prifon Com-
pound, but not out on't ;
he was very refpectful to us
Two, and would every Night
before he flept have fome
talk of Chriftianity and *England* ; his Age was about
Forty ; he was a pretty tall
and fpare Man, of a grave
Countenance ; he feemed to
be mightily taken with the
Laws and Cuftoms of the
Chri-

Christians. I cured one of
his Sons of the Itch, and
gave his Wife a Water to
wash her Eyes with, she being very dimsighted.

About the beginning of
this Month there came Five
Men hither in a Proe from
some of the Islands belonging to the King, their Business
was to the King's Son, who
was indebted to them for
some Service they had done
him, and from whom they
now expected their Recom-
pence in either Rice or Money; but he not answering
their Demands, they affront-
ed him with ill Language,
which so provok'd him that
he drew his Crease, and with
it wounded one of them,
whose Respect to his Prince
did not so far govern him
but

but that he repaid the
Wound in the fame Coin ;
at which they all drew their
Creafes, and had infallibly
kill'd him, had not a parcel
of Boys kept them in play
till the Town was alarm'd ;
immediately moft of the Houfes were fhut, and all the
Men run Arm'd with Laun-
ces and Creafes, fome to the
King's Compound, and fome
to *Datto Bandaro*'s ; and notwithftanding there were Several Hundreds of Arm'd Men
in and about the King's Compound, they kill'd but One of
the Fellows, and tock Three
Prifoners, the other made his
Way through the thickeft of
them into the Woods ; none
of them offer'd to follow
him, but ftill kept on their
Guards, and their Doors
close

clofe fhut; at which wondring Anno
I ask'd why (fince One was 1703.
kill'd, Three taken Prifoners,
and the Fifth ran away,)
they ftill kept fo ftrict a
Guard? And received for
Anfwer, That tho' he then
ran away, he would return
again, and kill all he could,
till fome Body put a ftop to
his Fury, by giving him his
Death, and accordingly a-
bout Five *P. M.* he returned
with his drawn Creafe to the
King's Palace, and tho' Hundreds ftood Arm'd all round
him, they none of them
dar'd venture to feize or af-
fault him, nor did he offer
at any of them, as if he fcorn'd
any thing lefs than a Prince;
it being him at whom he
aim'd his Revenge, and for
whom he made a fruitlefs
Search,

Search, while the Arm'd
Men fheer'd from him, (like
fo many Sheep before a
Wolf) to give him room
to range in. At laft being
tired with fearching for one
who was fafely enough fe-
cured from his Rage, he fat
him down on a Block clofe
by his Dead Comrade, up-
on which they fuddenly
ftruck a great Number of
Launces into him, and dif-
patcht him fitting, they not
thinking their fo exceeding
difparity in Number Ad-
vantage fufficient while he
was in a pofture of Defence ;
after which, like Brave Fellows, they marched Home,
and fearlefly fet open their
Houfes again ; and thus ended the mighty Fray. While
the Prince lay ill of his
Wound,

Wound, abundance of Wo- men went every Day to cry over and bemoan him ; and feveral of the Natives would have perfwaded me to offer my Service towards his Cure, but upon Information that whether I cured or killed him my Life would be e- qually in Danger from their Priefts, whofe Bufinefs that was, I avoided the Employ, by faying I did not under- ftand thofe Cures.

On the 9th of this Month it happened that a *Malaya* and a *Macaffer* fell out in their Play for a Woman ; it being cuftomary among thefe People not only to game away their Money, Houfes,*&c.* but their Wives, Children, and Concubines too ; the Quarrel grew to

that

Anno
1703.

that height, that the *Macaffer* Man ftabb'd the *Malayan*
in 8 or 9 Places, and killed
him, which done he let fall
his Hair, and with his drawn
Creafe made his Way to-
ward the King's Palace, accompanied by 6 or 7 more
of his Countrymen, who
had all likewife let fall their
Hair, and Arm'd themfelves
with Creafes and Launces;
upon which, abundance of
Malaya's likewife Arm'd
themfelves, but without offering to moleft them, or im-
pede their Progrefs; being
come before the King, they
acquainted him with what
had paffed, and were by him
pardoned for the Murther.
I have feveral times feen this
Man walk about Town, but
not without 2 or 3 of his
Coun-

Country men with him. It
is remarkable, that when the
Men let down their Hair,
(which they always wear
knotted up behind,) they are
desperately resolved to go
through with their Designs.
An Example of their Brave-
ry our selves have had on
the Island of *Borneo*, where
if they had not performed
the Parts of Men, the *Ban-
gereen* had it's thought taken the Factory, and cut off
all the *English*, about the
time *Datto Bandaro* was taken Sick.

On the 15th the *Supply*
Sloop came hither, whereof
Mr. *Hall* was Merchant, and
Mr. *Clifton* Captain ; we had
heard of her Arrival over
Night in the River, and at
8 this Morning *Packet* with
Mr.

Mr. *Bright* had been aboard, came to tell me that the Captain knew me very well, and defired to fee me ; accordingly my Comrade and I went to pay our Refpects to him and the Merchant, with whom we found the other Three; we were all Five kindly treated with Pork and Punch, at that time a very great Rarity. This Evening Mr. *Hall* told us he would get us all New Cloaths next Morning, and was as good as his Word, and promifed it fhould not be long e'er we had our Liberty if One or Two Hundred Dollars would procure it, for which kind Profers we returned him our Humble Thanks. We could not but think it an extraordinary Providence of God

God in sending so worthy-
minded a Friend to our Relief, who might have been
put to Death or Circumci-
sed had he been as base as
many are. We staid on Board
the Sloop till the 17th, being
treated all the time by Mr.
Hall; in the Morning we
went ashore, and when we
came Home miss'd our Mats,
Pillows, *&c.* which occasioned a small Surprize till I
remembred I had given them
into the Charge of the
Prisoner beforementioned;
whereupon I bid *Bremeridge*
look into his Partition, which
was made with Redjans, in
the same Room he saw the
Things, but cry'd out, the
Man is gone, and has taken
his Things along with him;
at which while we were re-
joicing,

Anno joicing, and faying he was an
1703. Honeft Man for taking fo
much Care of our Things
before he went away, in
came a young Lad, who holding up his Hands, and fhaking
his Head, told us that both
the Man and Woman had
been put to Death very early
in the Morning, at which being very much furpriz'd we
feem'd to doubt of the Truth,
till it was confirmed by 2
or 3 more, who all told us
that about 2 in the Morning
the Captain of the *Bailile*
came to him, and told him
that he had *Datto Bandaro*'s
Order for his and his Wives
immediate Death; that he received his Sentence with
great Content, only begging
of them to fend for us Two,
whom he was very urgent to
fee

see before his Death ; but the
Captain told him it could
not be ; that his Order was
to take his Life now while it
was the Hour of the Moon's
Full, and forthwith ordered
him to be carried to the Place
of Execution ; where he let
fall some Tears ; but told the
Standers-by it was not for
fear of Death, but because
they would not send for us
Two, whom he long'd to
see once more.　The fore-
said Captain *Datto Poonurlas*
was his Executioner, by running a Crease into his Body,
(as we stick Pigs,) on the Left
Side, between his Collar-bone
and Neck ; his Wife was
put to Death by having a
Stone made fast about her
Neck, and being thrown
out of a Proe into the River.

F

ver. I never could hear what their Crimes were, nor can I guess at any, except it was the Report they had of being Rich ; it being the Custom of this Country for *Datto Bandaro* to seize into his Hands all the Effects of any Delinquents that suffer Death.

Toward the latter End of this Month *Datto Bandaro* (who had been taken Sick on the 9th) made his Publick Appearance, and Mr. *Hall* sent his Linguister to demand us, and know the Reason why he detain'd us, but was put off 3 or 4 times without any Answer to the Purpose ; till at last being prest by Mr. *Hall* himself, he agreed to release us for 200 Dollars, which was promised him, and for which we again retur-

turned our Hearty Thanks
to Mr. *Hall*; but defired him
not to feem too eager, and
peradventure he might procure our Freedom at an eafier Rate. At that time he
told us, that tho' he could
not at prefent do for us all,
yet it would not be long
firft; that in the mean time
we were all welcome on
Board the Sloop to Eat and
Drink as he did; where finding Plenty of Punch and
Rack, from which we had before been for a long debar-
red, and by confequence could
not bear fo much as we had
been ufed to do, we fell into
Debates and Controverfies a-
mong our felves, which (tho'
very difpleafing to Mr. *Hall*,)
did not avert his Kindneffes
to us, he only faying, he defired us to agree among our

F 2   felves.

selves. The Remainder of
the Month we liv'd on Board
the Sloop, having Money of
Mr. *Hall*.

At the beginning of this
Month a *Malaya* Man was
killed in the Act of Adulte-
ry. Mr. *Hall* was busied in
procuring his Lading, and
about the middle of the
Month the *Baylile* was filled
with Prisoners. Near the
same time as I was walking
in the Town a *Malayan* ask'd
me whither the Captain
would Buy any Ambergreafe?
Saying he had above 3 Cad-
dy or Pounds, which he had
taken up as he was going to
Camboidia ; I told him, if I
thought it good I would carry
him to Mr. *Hall*, who would
give him either Gold or *Opium*.
He told me he would show
it me, but desired me not to
men-

Anno
1702.

mention it to any other *Malayan,* which I promifed, and
went home with him to fee
it ; where being come he
put fome into the Fire with
a piece of Wood of a Light
Green Colour, which gave
a very pleafant Odour ;
from thence I carried him
aboard the Sloop to Mr. *Hall* ;
he would not venture to carry it himfelf, but gave it me
to carry for him. Mr. *Hall*
having try'd a little of it,
faid he did not think it was
good, but bid the Man ftay
till his Linguifter came, who
knew it better than himfelf ;
who was no fooner come a-
board, but faid it was adul-
terated with Bees-Wax ; the
Smell of it was rather Offen-
five than Pleafant, and its
Colour refembling that of

F 3   Salt

Salt Beef Suit; it was of the hardnefs of a foft Mellow Cheefe, and was tough and greafie, and within ftringy; fome of it laid on a piece of white Paper, and melted, gave a good fcent, and leaving the Drofs behind dry'd into the Paper.

I believe if I make a fmall Digreffion to relate a Story concerning the Nature of Ambergreafe it may not be amifs. One Day as I was talking with my Father concerning thofe Fellows that adulterate Ambergreafe he told me the *Melaya*'s cou'd not do it, but that it was the Inhabitants of *Camboidia* and *Cochin-China* only did it; and withal fell into the Story. In the late King's Reign I was fent about Bufinefs to a

Place

Place on the Main about 4
Days Sail to the Northward
of *Jehore*, where I saw some
People belonging to the
Captain *De Quallo*, who were
rubbing the Bottoms of Two
Proes with Ambergreafe ; I
asked them what they did that
for? their Anfwer was, to make
them run faft ; upon which
I took it off the Ground,
and gave them a new Arfe-
clout for it, telling them I had
a better ufe for it at *Jehore*;
they receiv'd the Cloth with
abundance of Thanks, and
feeming fatisfaction ; when I
came to *Jehore* I prefented
the greateft part of it to the
King. This Story being ended,
I defired him to give an Account of it, and tell me how
I fhould know it, which he
begun thus ; it is a flimly
F 4　　　Stuff

Anno
1703.

Stuff vomited by a certain great Fiſh, and drives about on the Surface of the Water till ſwallowed by another Fiſh, who very greedily eats it, tho' it will not ſtay in his Stomach, no Fiſh in the Sea being able to digeſt it. If it happens to drive aſhore before it has been thus eaten and vomited up Seven times it is not at its right Perfection, but is ſoft, ſlimy, and its Smell not ſo ſtrong as whenSeven times ſwallowed, which brings it to its full Perfection; and if it then drives aſhore is found by its Smell, which is ſo ſtrong as not to ſuffer it to be hid, and which draws to it abundance of Vermine, as Ants and Auguſts, (*i. e.*) ſmall Flies; and then taking a piece of White
Silk,

Silk, he rubb'd Tobacco Ashes on it, and show'd it me for the Colour of it; I ask'd what fort of Smell it had? He after a little Paufe told me it was to fome Men not very plea-fing, but to others of a fresh and fragant Smell. Toward the latter End of the Month the *Portugueze* Sloop fell down the River, bound for *Camboidia*; feveral of his *Laf-cars* having left him, he took *Chinois* and *Malayans* in their Room. *Edward Bethall* had agreed to go his Boatfwain; but his Mind being altered, Mr. *Hall* repaid the Money he had received. About this time Mr. *Hall* Bought a Northern Sloop, (much big-ger than his own,) of the *Chi-na* Men; he gave 18 Hun-dred Dollars for her Cargo,

F 5   which.

which was 50c Peculls of Sugar.

August 3d Arrived here a Country Ship belonging to *Delton*, *John Monkester* Commander, from *Achein* ; the same Evening Mr. *Hall* fell down the River in the *Supply* Sloop, bound for *Mallacca* ; he took with him Mr. *Bright* and *Bremeridge*, leaving my self and the other Two on Board the Sloop he had Bought, with his Brother Linguifter, an *Armenian*, and 3 Black *Portugueze* more ; he defired us to give our Attendance to his Sloop, in the Night efpecially, and ordered his Linguifter to let us have any thing in Reafon that we wanted. On the 10th we had an Account that the

Por-

Portugueze Sloop was run a-
way with, and the Christians barbaroufly Murthered,
and their Bodies taken up a
very little to the Northward
of the River's Mouth.   On
the 24th the King was taken
very Ill, and continued fo
this Month.

September 2. came down
the River 4 very large Proes,
and a fmall one at fome diftance after them ; they were
adorn'd with Silk Colours,
furnifh'd with abundance of
the Country Mufick , and
fili'd with Men and Women, who where employ-
ed in Singing and tending
the Fires, which the Men
with loud fhouting and hal-
lowing threw it into the Air,
and at 5 *Ditto* return'd again,
rowing directly to the King's
Palace.

Palace. They had been (as
we were informed) to re-
turn thanks to the Devil,
and make him Prefents for
the King's Recovery, and to
procure more *Oback* ; which
is the Name for all Medi-
cines or Salves to whatever
Diftemper applyed ; as *Oback*
for the Eyes, *Oback* to caufe
Sweating, and *Opack Merium,* (*i. e.*) Gunpowder. On
the 4th the King's Sifter, who
was Wife to the *Shebander,*
died in Childbed. On the
6th Mr. *Hall* arrived from
Malacca, bringing with him
befides our Two Comrades
one Mr. *Heriott,* who belonged to the *Scotch* Ship loft in
the Streights of *Malacca.* In
the Evening the *Shebander's*
Wife was Buried with great
Solemnity ; moft part of the
City

City went into Mourning for
her, which they do by sha-
ving their Heads, and tying
a String of white Cotton
twisted about them ; their
Mourning Cloaths are Red,
White, and Blue, and envi-
roned with so great variety
of Fancies, that it's rare to see
Two alike.　Her Grave was
for several Days after visited
by a great many Young
Girles singing over it.　The
8th Mr. *Hall* named his new
Sloop the *Increase*, and toward the latter End of the
Month fell down with both
the Sloops to *Jehore Lama*,
(*i. e.*) *Old Jehore*, to lay
them ashore, and repair
them.

October 6th a *Malayan* Man
and his Wife were put to
Death by *Datto Bandaro's*
　　　　　　　　Or-

Anno
1703.

Order ; becaufe (according to his own Report) during the time of his Sicknefs, whenever he flept or flumber'd, this Man and his Wife would appear to him, and taking him by the Throat, endeavour to ftrangle him. On the 7th Mr. *Hall* told us he had procured our Freedom by a Letter to *Datto Bandaro* from the Governour of *Malacca*, whom the *Malayans* call the *Raja*, or King of *Malacca*.

In the beginning of this Month Mr. *Hall* and his Two Sloops lying at *Jehore Lame* the one afhore, and the Sloop *Increafe* lying as Guard-Sloop ; the *Supply* was repair'd, and then the *Increafe* hawl'd afhore here, and refitted. During our ftay at *Jehore bore Lame* Mr. *Hall* got the Master of the Ship *Good Fortune* clear ; which Captain *Monkester* was very free to agree to, upon the Account that he should have one of us in his Room. Mr. *Hall* obtained his Defire, and brought him down, and gave him the Charge of feeing his Veffel repair'd ; upon which my felf, *George Bright,* and *John Bremeridge,* defired that we might be clear of him ; and telling him we would apply our felves to the Captain of their Ship, and he had not loft by entertaining us aboard his Sloops, we would appeal to any Man if we had not doubly earned whatever he had done for us ; withal telling him, if his Pleafure was to make the

very

very worft of us all Five the
Mafter of his Sloop *Increafe*,
his Work fhould go forward
as well as his Heart could
defire; but it was ill for him to
make Promifes fo fair to us,
telling us he would not
put any Man over our Heads
as long as we were capable
of thofe Imploys, and fo
foon to falfifie his Word
with us; we told him, that
tho' we were under this dark
and hazey Sky at that time,
fome of us had been in much
better Employs than the Man
he had opened his Pocket fo
largely to, and were abun-
dantly more capable of the
Employ; but our Poverty is fo
great it changes our Looks,
having the hard Fate that ne-
verany *Englifhman* met with
in that remote Country of the
Ma-

Malaya's, and more especial-
ly in the Dominions of the
King of *Jehore.* I believe
those *Englishmen* that are acquainted in those Parts with
the *Malaya*'s People will allow it a great Providence of
God that we have been so
strangely preserved. However, Mr. *Hall* said, it is my
Pleasure he shall come here
and have the Charge ; so we
3 bowed, and took our leaves
of him, and walking down
the River side to the Town of
Jehore Lame before we were
out of Sight ; he sent a Man
to tell us he desired to speak
to us once more ; so back
we 3 went to know his Will,
who said, Gentlemen. what
would you have ? We told
him he knew our Grievance
without any longer Talk ;
                              then

then he said, Gentlemen, I
promise you he shan't be your
Master ; and whatever you
want speak to me for it ; and
then he spoke to Mr. *Vaughan*,
*I hope you will forward my
Business , for I trust to you.*
Now all things went clearly
on, and the Sloop had a
heal again, and got on a
false Keel, and Work went
forward with a willing Mind ;
but in 9 Days time Mr. *Hall*
forgot all this, and brought
the same Man down. In the
beginning of this Month
Mr. *Hall* turn'd away the Master of his Old Sloop *Supply*,
and told him he would give
him an Account of what
was done when he requested
it.

A

A True Copy of a Let-
ter that I writ by the
Requeft of my other
4 Comrades, and was
delivered to one Bea-
go *a* Chinaman *for*
to be carried to Ma-
lacca, *but I believe*
was carried to Amoy
in China *by the fame*
Junk that he belonged
to.

' T H E S E are to Cer-
' tifie all Chriftian
' People, Prefidents, Com-
' manders,and others belong-
' ing to the *Englifh* Nation,
                    ' that

'that there are now at *Jehore*
' 5 poor Souls, Servants to
' the *New-Company*, being
' drove from the Island of
' *Pulo Condore* by a hard
' Storm of Wind, in a small
' Proe, in passing from the
' Harbour to the Facto-
' ry, with 4 Guns, a But of
' Lime, Huddles, and a Ca-
' nister of Sugar. On the 19th
' Day of *January* 1703 we
' went out of the same Har-
' bour of *Pulo Condore*, from
' on Board the Ship *Safe-
' guard*, to turn up to the
' Factory; and on the 20th of
' *January* we were forc'd off,
' our Anchor not holding us,
' and on the 29th of the
' same Instant were drove
' ashore at a Place call'd *In-
' dowe*, belonging to the King
'of

' of *Jehore*, and there being Anno
' detained till the 18th of 1703.
' *March* 1703, at which
' time we were put on Board
' the Proe, with one of
' their Great Men or Captain,
' and Four more of the Na-
' tives, and on the 19th of
' the fame Inftant arrived
' at the Town of *New Jehore*
' about 9 in the Night, and
' the next Day in the Morn-
' ing carried before the King
' of *Jehore*, of whom we de-
' fired to let us pafs for *Ma-
' lacca*, who would not, his
' Nobles and himfelf preffing
' us to turn *Malaya*'s; and
' telling us if we did not
' they would cut off our
' Heads, or Creafe us; yet
' we would not confent to
' their Wicked Defire, and
' Hope

' Hope that God will give
' us his Grace, and so strong
' a Faith, as not to fear dy-
' ing for him, since he suf-
' fered his Son Jesus Christ
' to die for us, and all Chri-
' stians ; that our Faith in his
' Mercy will make us chuse
' Death rather than such a
' Disgrace should happen to
' the Christians, and particu-
' larly those of the Church
' of *England* ; and pray to
' God for our happy Re-
' leasement by some good
' Ship, or else of your Ho-
' nourable Hands, which if
' it happens we shall give
' a particular Account of the
' Hardships undergone by us
' Five Miserable Souls, whose
' Names are hereunder writ-
' ten, and all *Englishmen*,
                        ' and

' and reft your poor diftreffed
' Servants,

George Bright, } Steward of the Factory of *Pulo Condore,* and the Charge of the Boat.

Walter Vaughan,
Edward Bethall,
John Bremeridge,
Nathaniel Packet, } Belonging to the Ship *Safe-Guardas* Four here mentioned.

When drove from the Ifland of *Pulo Condore* we neither had Water nor Food, the Oldeft of us Five not paffing 26 Years of Age. The want of Paper and Pens will not admit me to give a larger Account of this.

A

Anno
1703.

A Description of the King of Jehore's Palace.

IT is a large irregular Square, Built with great Logs of Wood, or Piles set an end in the Ground close to one another, and about 16 Foot high; within 4 Foot of the top there is a Gallery 6 Foot broad, built quite round it for his Men to stand on; on the top of the Piles are placed Brass Ramtackers in Swivels, about 5 Yards one from the other, that carry a Ball of a Pound Weight; below are Ports cut at a convenient distance, to run Guns out at, some of which are supplied, but the greateft

eft are altogether ufelefs.

The River of *Jehore* runs by the City of that Name, which is the Seat of that little Kingdom, which lyes on the Continent of *Malacca*. It abounds with Pepper, and other good Commodities. They are a *Mahometan* People, very Warlike, and inclining to Trade, delighting much in Shipping, and going to Sea, all the Neighbouring Iflands in a Manner being Colonies of this Kingdom. They coaft about in their own Shipping to feveral Parts of *Jara, Sumatra,* &c. Their Veffels are but fmall, yet very Serviceable; and the *Dutch* buy up a great many of them at a fmall Price, and make good Sloops of them. But they firft fit them up after their own Fafhion, and put a Rudder to them, which the *Jeborians* do not ufe, tho' they are very good Seamen in their Way; but they make their Veffels fharp

G   at

Anno 1703. at each End, tho' but One End is us'd as the Head, and instead of a Rudder they have on each Side the Stern a Thing like a broad Oar, One of which they let down into the Water at Pleasure, as there is Occasion to steer the Ship, on the one Side or the other, always letting down that which is to the Leeward. They have Proes of a particular Neatness and Curiosity; we call them Half-moon Proes, for they turn up so much at each End from the Water, that they much resemble a Half-moon, with the Horns upwards. They are kept very clear, and Sail well, and are much used by them in their Wars. The People of *Jehore* have formerly endeavoured to get a Commerce with our Nation; but that Trade seems to be much neglected by us. The *Dutch* trade very much here, and have lately endeavoured to bring over their King, who

is

is very Young, wholly to their
Interest. And so much for this
little Kingdom of *Jehore*.

By the Letter formerly mentioned, and other Application
made by us, a Vessel arrived at
Length from *Malacca*, and took
us all in: So that after all the
Sorrows, Fears, and Dangers,
wherewith we had been exer-
cised for so long a Time, we
were Landed safely at *Pulo Condore*, the Place from whence we
were driven to this Countrey.

I shall conclude with giving
some Account of *Pulo Condore*,
which is the Principal of an
Heap of Islands, lying in 8
Degrees, 5 Minutes North La-
titude, about 15 Miles Long,
and 3 Miles Broad. There is
a Sort of Tree much bigger
than any other, and not commonly seen elsewhere; it is 3
or 4 Foot Diameter in the Body, from whence is drawn a
Sort of Clammy Juice, which

G 2　　　being

being boil'd a little becomes
perfect Tarr, and if boil'd much
will be as hard as Pitch, and is
found very serviceable if ufed
either Way. The Fruit Trees
that Nature has beftow'd on
thefe Ifles are *Mango's* which
grow on Trees as big as Apple-
trees; when ripe they have fo
delicate a Fragrancy, that we
can fmell them at Sea from the
thick Woods, if we have but
Wind of them, tho' we could
not fee them. The Grape-tree
grows in a ftrait Body, about a
Foot round, and hath but a few
Limbs or Boughs. The Fruit
grows in Clufters about the Body of the Tree, fome of them
Red, others White: They are
much like fuch Grapes as grow
on our Vines, both in Grape and
Colour, and of a very pleafant
Winy Tafte. The Wild Nut-
meg-tree is as big as a Walnut-
tree; but it does not fpread fo
much; the Boughs are long, and
the

theFruit grows among theBoughs, as the Walnut, and other Fruits. It is much smaller than the true Nutmeg, and longer also ; it is inclos'd in a thin Shell, and a sort of Mace incircling the Nut within the Shell. This Bastard Nutmeg is is so like the true One in Shape, that when first arrived here, we thought it to be the true One, but it has no manner of Smell nor Taste.

The Animals of this Island are some Hogs, Lizards, and Guanoes, Horses, Bulls, Cows, Buffuloes, Goats, Wild Hogs, Deer, Monkies, Snakes ; I never saw nor heard of any Beasts of Prey here, as in many other Places. The Hogs are ugly Creatures ; they have all great Knobs growing over their Eyes, and there are Multitudes of them in the Woods. They are commonly very Poor, yet sweet : Here are many Sorts of Birds, as Parrots, Parahites, Doves, Pigeons ; there

are

are alſo a Wild Sort of Cocks
and Hens; they are much like
our tame Fowl of that Kind, but
a great deal leſs about the Bigneſs of a Crow; the Cocks crow
like ours, but much more ſmall
and ſhrill, and by that we find
them out, and ſhoot them in the
Woods; their Fleſh is very
White and Sweet.

This Iſland lyes very commo-
diouſly for refreſhing and remit-
ting Ships from the *Eaſt Indies*,
where they may be furniſhed
with Maſts, Yards, Pitch, and
Tarr. The Inhabitants are but
ſmall of Stature, well enough
ſhaped, and of a darkiſh Colour; they are pretty long viſag-
ed; their Hair is Black and Strait,
their Eyes Small and Black, their
Noſes of a mean Bigneſs, and
ſomewhat High, their LipsThin,
their Teeth White, and Little
Mouths; they are ſo free of
their Women, that they bring
them aboard, and offer them to
Stran-

Strangers, of whom the Women
are very fond, and may be hired
for a fmall Matter. This is a
Cuftom likewife ufed by feveral
Nations in the *Eaft-Indies*, as at
Pegu, *Siam*, and *Tonquin*, where
moft of the Seamen take Women
aboard while they lye in Harbour; and on the Coaft of *Guinea* our Men have their Black
Miffes, it being accounted a
Piece of Policy to do it; for the
chief Factors and Captains of
Ships have the Great Men's
Daughters, yea, the Noblemen's
in fome Places offered to them,
and even the King's Wives in
Guinea; and by this Sort of Alliance the Slaves are engaged to
a greater Friendfhip: And if
there fhould arife any Difference
about Trade, or any Thing elfe,
which might provoke the Inhabitants to feek fome Treacherous
Revenge; (to which all thefe
HeathenNations are much prone)
thefe *Dalilah's*, or *Pugallies*, as
they